U0033847

台灣原住民的神話與傳說〈①〉泰雅族、布農族、鄒族

Taiwan Indigene : Meaning Through Stories : Atayal, Bunun, Tsou

總 策 劃	孫大川	英文翻譯	文魯彬
故事採集	里慕依・阿紀	繪　　圖	瑁瑁・瑪邵
	阿浪・滿拉旺		陳景生
	巴蘇亞・迪亞卡納		阿伐伊・尤干伐那

社　　長	洪美華	責任編輯	謝宜芸、何喬
初版協力	曾麗芬、林玉珮、林宜妙	美術設計	蔡靜玫
	劉秀芬、黃信瑜	封面設計	盧穎作
		市場行政	莊佩璇、巫毓麗、黃麗珍、洪美月

出　　版　幸福綠光股份有限公司
　　　　　台北市杭州南路一段 63 號 9 樓
　　　　　(02)2392-5338
　　　　　www.thirdnature.com.tw

E - m a i l ： reader@thirdnature.com.tw
印　　製：中原造像股份有限公司
新　　版：2021 年 10 月
郵撥帳號：50130123 幸福綠光股份有限公司
定　　價：新台幣 550 元 (平裝)

總經銷　　聯合發行股份有限公司
　　　　　新北市新店區寶橋路
　　　　　235 巷 6 弄 6 號 2 樓
　　　　　(02)2917-8022

國家圖書館出版品預行編目資料

台灣原住民的神話與傳說（1）：泰雅族、
布農族、鄒族／瑁瑁・瑪邵等著 . -- 初版 .
-- 臺北市：幸福綠光，2021.10
　　面；公分
ISBN 978-986-06748-3-5（平裝）

863.859　　　　　　　　　110011327

台灣原住民的神話與傳說

Taiwan Indigene : Meaning Through Stories : Atayal, Bunun, Tsou

泰雅族、布農族、鄒族

故事採集　里慕依·阿紀／阿浪·滿拉旺／巴蘇亞·迪亞卡納

繪　圖　瓃瓃·瑪邵／陳景生／阿伐伊·尤干伐那

總 策 劃　孫大川

英文翻譯　文魯彬

①

CONTENTS｜目次

彩繪原畫欣賞

第一冊　泰雅族、布農族、鄒族

1. 泰雅族 Atayal

2. 布農族 Bunun

3. 鄒族 Tsou

4. 部落百寶盒　Treasure Box of the Tribes

非看不可的原住民資料庫

族語開口說　　　造訪部落
Learn the　　　Visit the Tribes
Languages

＊ 本套書共三冊，二、三冊目錄如後。

第二冊　阿美族、卑南族、達悟族

1. 阿美族 Amis

2. 卑南族 Puyuma

3. 達悟族 Tao

非看不可的原住民資料庫

族語開口説
Learn the
Languages

造訪部落
Visit the Tribes

第三冊　魯凱族、排灣族、賽夏族、邵族

3. 賽夏族 Saisiyat

4. 邵族 Thao

非看不可的原住民資料庫

- 造訪部落　　魯凱、排灣、賽夏、邵
- 族語開口說　魯凱、排灣、賽夏、邵
- 學習加油站　魯凱、排灣、賽夏、邵
- 挑戰 Q&A
- E 網情報站
- 製作群亮相

族語開口説　　　造訪部落
Learn the　　　Visit the Tribes
Languages

2021 推薦語　以神話與傳說承載原住民歷史 （依姓氏筆劃排序）

Saidhai

1996年，我回到母校繼續碩士學程。當時寫論文，為了什麼主題煩惱不已。指導教授提醒我，萬丈高樓平地起，既是決定未來往原住民族議題研究發展，應當從原住民族文化的文本分析奠定良基。

這套《台灣原住民的神話與傳說》，對於許多想要認識原住民文化的朋友，或者從事原住民研究的學生，甚至是原住民本身，這是最重要也是最基礎的入門書。

在電子出版蓬勃的時代，特別感佩幸福綠光出版社以精緻的重編再版這套叢書。期盼這樣的心意，喞來更多的新枝，豐富神的花園。

（伍麗華／校長立委）

原住民神話不只是原住民族文學心靈的泉源，也是延伸台灣人民共同想像空間的資源。這本書將原住民神話配以精緻的圖畫，不但可讀性甚高，而且提供很多延伸閱讀的資訊，誠為認識原住民文化的駿良入門書。

（吳密察／台灣史學者‧國立故宮博物院院長）

Ara‧Kimbo

神話與傳說乃人類歷史之母，口述的神話與傳說是台灣原住民歷史的脈絡，更是台灣史之根源。

身為台灣人不可不溫習自己的神話傳說，熟悉自己的歷史。

（胡德夫／民歌之父‧原權會創會會長）

陳耀昌

《斯卡羅》掀起「探討台灣史」、「了解原住民」的全民運動，讓我們深刻領悟，台灣是「多元族群、同島一命」：

- 原住民了解白浪，白浪卻不夠了解原住民。
- 您知道嗎？台灣原住民是南島語族的祖先，台灣原住民是台灣帶給世界的禮物。
- 了解原住民，請從了解原住民祖先的神話與傳說開始。
- 何況，天啊！《魯凱族》的插畫竟然出自原住民大藝術家：伊誕‧巴瓦瓦隆，太珍貴了。

（陳耀昌／醫師‧名作家）

薛化元

每個民族/族群都有長久流傳的神話與傳說。

神話與傳說雖不是歷史，卻是民族/族群歷史記憶的展現。因此，神話與傳說也成為重要的歷史文化資產。

台灣原住民由於早期沒有文字，神話與傳說更承載了原住民的歷史傳承，而這也是這套書價值之所在。

（薛化元／政治大學台灣史研究所教授）

初版推薦語

總策劃序　關心原住民議題的重要入門書

這一套10冊的《台灣原住民的神話與傳說》，集合了原住民的作者與畫者，出版於2002年年底，初版、二版都刷了好幾刷，雖談不上暢銷，但長期以來，它仍然是關心原住民議題的讀者重要的入門書。

2016年，出版社更投入心力，封面、紙張做了更新。在族語語彙的拼法，無法全面改成和現行官方書寫系統一致的情況下，編者們設計了「開口說」的音檔，以掃描 QR Code 的方式（見目錄），直接讓讀者聆聽族語，用聲音拉近彼此的距離。

尤其，2001年之後，原住民各族的正名訴求紛紛獲得官方的認定，目前台灣原住民已經分為16族了，這是我們在人權上很大的進步。這些新認定的族群有葛瑪蘭族（Kebalan，2002）、太魯閣族（Truku，2004）、撒奇萊雅族（Sakizaya，2007）、賽德克族（Seedig，2008）、拉阿魯哇族（Hla'alua，2014）、卡那卡那富族（Kanakanavu，2014）等6族；連同近年來愈來愈受到矚目的平埔族各族正名運動，反映了原住民議題發展的新趨勢。我們真誠的希望親愛的讀者們，能注意這些變化，更深地了解我們原住民的族人。

我們十分珍惜這套《台灣原住民的神話與傳說》系列所積累的將近20年的文化資產記憶，幾經考慮，出版社決定重新編排再版，在不減損其豐富內容的前提下，將原本10冊的規模濃縮成3冊的形式，以降低書籍的成本，嘉惠更多的讀者。我們這次雖然仍沒有能力增補後來正名的6族，但這幾年也看到不少有關他們，包括平埔族，相當豐富的出版物，熱心的讀者應該可以從其他管道掌握與他們相關的資訊，彌補我們的缺憾。

要特別指出的是，這次我們在插畫的處理上做了重大的變革。經幾比對，我們發現插圖用黑白呈現，不但可以避免色彩喧賓奪主的情況，而且反而更能突顯整體畫面細膩的線條與素樸古雅的風格。不過，對彩色有興趣的讀者，仍可用QR Code找到原畫的初貌。尤其，更值得一提的是，我們這套書的英文譯者文魯彬先生（Robin Winkler），在台灣生活近40年，深入認識了台灣，並更走進了原住民的世界，他以極大的熱情重新潤飾他原來的故事英譯，還增加了「What's more?」和「Where did it come from?」等內容。我們希望有更多外國朋友，透過這套書打開的窗口，認識優美的原住民文化！

An Easy Book to Enter the World of Tribes

The "Taiwan Indigene: Meaning Through Stories," a collection of writings and paintings by Taiwanese indigenous peoples, was first published at the end of 2002. The original and many reprints of the series, while not a "best seller," is established as an excellent introduction for those interested in the indigene of Taiwan. The 2016 edition even included a QR code link for those wishing to hear the vocabulary of the indigenous languages.

Following the series' release in 2002, years of struggle by many of Taiwanese indigenous peoples bore fruit, and the ten tribes recognized when the series was first published, grew to 16 officially recognized tribes. The six new tribes and their year of official recognition are the Kebalan (2002), Truku (2004), Sakizaya (2007), Sediq (2008), Hla'alua (2014) and Kanakanavu (2014). The recognition of these tribes and attention given to the so called "plains tribes" all reflect the development of our nation's "indigene" dialog. We sincerely hope these stories will help our people to follow these trends and gain a deeper understanding of Taiwan's indigenous peoples and culture.

I treasure experiences over the past twenty years and was delighted with the publisher's decision to reissue the books with revised content and format. Without detracting from any of the original stories, the ten volumes have been combined into three so as to make the books accessible to a wider audience. As an aesthetic choice, we also decided to print this reissue with the paintings in black and white – the color paintings are available at our website. While no new stories were prepared for the six newly recognized tribes, we have included much new information about those tribes, as well as information for the as yet unrecognized plains tribes.

It is worth mentioning that the English translator for the series Robin Winker, has since the series' first release, spent considerable time immersed in Taiwan's indigenous culture, and for this series the translations have all been revised and new material has been added, notably the "What's more" sections. Through these stories we look forward to welcoming many more foreign readers to the richness of Taiwan's indigenous culture.

Paelabang danapan

泰 雅 族
A t a y a l

▷小筆記 ▶

・擅長織布、竹編、藤編手藝。
・分佈南投以北台灣整個北部山區,民族性堅定強悍。
・嘎嘎泛指泰雅族的一切規範,出草就是執行規範的意思。

・泰雅星群：徐若瑄、林慶台、陳盈潔、楊林、張雨生、高金素梅、曾之喬、言承旭、周渝民、溫嵐……。

・翻過中央山脈到花蓮的太魯閣族，於2004年被官方認定為第12個台灣原住民族、賽德克族則於2008年被認定為第14族。

故事導讀　神聖的祖訓

多民族的始祖傳說一樣，泰雅族祖先的來源絕對不是人類個別的行動，而是大地、宇宙的一個共同事件。

第一則故事「巨石傳說」中，讓我們了解到，巨石、陽光和風雨，皆有助於人類的創造，而創生後的人類，若要綿延流長也不能單獨達成的，他需要兩股不同的力量，相反相成，因而有了男女。兩性的社會不能是任意的，所以才有了紋面的故事，倫理就這樣被建立了起來。如果你不願面對生命的艱難和規範，就只好像那巨石迸裂後又走回去的男人，永遠無法真正的誕生。

有生必有死，我們的生命與生活不是徒然生而已，我們必須活出意義和價值。在「彩虹橋的審判」故事中，讓我們的死已成為另一個生命的開始，而它的種子卻深埋在我們活著的時候是不是真能按照卜大的訓誨過活？

在泰雅人的誡律中，貪念或許是最大的罪惡。在「神奇的呼喚術」故事中，既懶惰又貪婪的那個婦人，濫用祖先神奇的呼喚術，得寸進尺，切下了山豬的耳朵、得罪了慷慨的稻米；而那惡作劇的年輕男子，也嚇跑了樂於幫人的木柴。破壞了人與大自然、人與萬物的和諧及倫理之後，其實人才是最大的受害者。

這就是泰雅祖訓的內涵，從「巨石傳說」、「神奇的呼喚術」到「彩虹橋的審判」，藉神話傳說的情節，深深地刻印在每一個泰雅人的身上。神話傳說因而不是荒誕不經的憑空想像，而是泰雅人行為規範以及生活禁忌的軌儀，是神聖的祖訓（gaga）。

里慕伊‧阿紀以她特有的女性柔細，為我們敘述泰雅族的起源傳說，並輕鬆地告訴我們紋面的來源，以及泰雅族的種種誡律。神話傳說不像法律規條，它讓我們回到倫理的原始根源，看出它和我們人性的關聯。倫理因而是活出來的，而不是單單拿來遵守的。尤其重要的是：倫理牽涉的範圍不只在人與人之間，更觸及到自然和萬物；它其實有很深的宇宙根基。

Reader's Guide　　Sacred Ancestral Teachings

As with the ancient legends of many different ethnicities, the origin of the Atayal ancestors is absolutely not actions of human beings in isolation but rather joint creation events of the earth and the heavens.

In the first story "Legend of the Giant Stone", we learned how boulders, sunlight, the wind and the rain all contributed to the creation of humans. However, if these humans are to carry on their species, it cannot be done as one, but needs two different forces, opposite yet complimentary: thus we have man and woman. The socializing of the two genders however cannot be arbitrary, hence the story of the tattoos and the introduction of ethical behavior. If one is unable to face the difficulties and norms of living, it is just as the man who goes back to the crevice – his line will never take hold and propagate.

There is life, and therefore there must be death. Our very life and the way we live that life is not something that just happens and has no role in the "bigger picture." This requires that we live with meaning and with value. Hence the story of the "Rainbow's Judgment" shows how our death is the beginning of another life, the seeds of that new life buried deep within the lives we live now. Can we really live according to the instructions and wisdom of Buta, the rainbow incarnate?

To the Atayal way of thinking, greed may be the greatest of all crimes. In the story of the "Magical Summons", the lazy and greedy woman abused the magical summons that had been passed down since time immemorial. She had been graced with enough but demanded so much more. She cut off the ears of the boar, and insulted the generous rice; while the mischievous young man also frightened the firewood which was so helpful to humans. After destroying the harmony with nature, destroying the harmony with all beings and phenomena, we humans are actually the biggest losers.

So, whether in the Legend of the Stone, the Magical Summons or the Rainbow's Judgment, these gifts of wisdom passed down from the Atayal ancestors are deeply imprinted on the body of every Atayal. These stories are not absurd imaginations, but they show us the Atayal code of conduct, their taboos, the sacred ancestral precepts of living – they show us gaga.

Rimuy Aki uses her unique female sensitivity to narrate the origins of the Atayal, the source of the Atayal facial tattoos and the various mandates of the Atayal. Unlike laws and regulations, these stories - so-called myths and legends - bring us back to the original root of ethics and show how it relates with our nature. Ethical codes are living, and not just to be slavishly observed. Most important is to understand and feel that ethics is not simply a matter of codes for interpersonal relations among humans, rather it also touches nature and all phenomena and reflects of a deep cosmological foundation.

01

巨石傳說

當第一道曙光照射在山頂的巨石，轟隆一聲，巨石裂成兩半，泰雅族的祖先從石縫中誕生。他們互愛互敬，慢慢學會自然環境下的生活方式；並且從觀察動物中，了解繁衍下一代的意義與方法。

很久很久以前的遠古時代，大地上還沒有人類出現。台灣島上中央山脈中部，迎向陽光的山頂上，矗立著一顆巨大的岩石。

這顆巨石外表光滑細緻，渾然天成。春去秋來，迎朝陽、送晚霞，汲取日月精華，不知不覺過了千千萬萬年。

有一天，晨風徐徐吹來，第一道曙光，由東方山頂上射出，「唰！」正好照射在巨岩中央。

突然間，「轟隆！」一聲，巨岩從中裂開，分成兩半。

從裂開的石縫裡，走出了兩男一女。剛開始，他們對眼前的新世界有點怯生，不久，便好奇的到處走動，東看看，西看看，不斷地環顧四周圍的環境。

其中一名男子看到週遭有許多懸崖峭壁與叢林深湖，心想，生活在這樣的世界，一定非常辛苦；越想越害怕，便轉身快步走回巨岩，並迅速跨入裂縫中。

走在稍遠處的另一對男女看到他走回巨石，大吃一驚，趕緊跑了過去，希望能將他留下，三人一起過生活。

就在這時候，忽然「嘎～～」的一聲，分裂的巨石迅速合併起來，恢復原來的樣子，彷彿從未發生過什麼變化似的，走回巨石的那位男子已經不見蹤影。

What's more?

傳說中巨石所在地：位於現在南投縣仁愛鄉發祥村瑞岩部落的山區，泰雅語稱為賓斯巴幹（pinsebugan），如今還可見到傳說中的石壁遺跡。pinsebugan是「分裂、裂開」的意思，傳說中巨岩分裂，生出了泰雅族祖先。

懸崖峭壁與叢林深湖：泰雅族傳統的生活領域大都位在海拔二、三千公尺以上的高山，叢林茂密，形勢險峻。

這對男女，只好默默的接受這個事實，從此結伴相依為命。

他們居住在高山叢林，平時以採集野菜、蔬果維生。身強力壯的男子經常上山下水獵捕山鹿、野兔、魚蝦等；手藝精巧的女子就拿獸皮縫製衣物，來遮蔽身體抵禦寒冷。

空閒的時候，他們喜歡坐在樹下，觀看梅花鹿在林間自由奔馳，細細聆聽樹上鳥兒啾啾鳴唱的歌聲。

大地是如此的寧靜、祥和，這對男女最喜歡做的事就是觀察動物的行為及習性，學習牠們如何在大自然中生存。

山林中的歲月就這麼日復一日地度過，生活悠閒而快活。但是，當他們在觀察各種動物的時候，發現牠們可以自然地繁衍下一代，令他們感到無比的好奇。

樹梢的鳥巢，一顆顆小巧的鳥蛋，過沒幾天就有四、五隻小鳥破殼而出，讓他們感到興奮不已。

梅花鹿猶如山中的精靈，靈巧的在林間穿梭奔跑。不時還會看見鹿媽媽，帶著撒嬌的小鹿跑上跑下，令他們心生憐惜。

倒地的枯樹下，常有成群的螞蟻列隊齊步走，合力扛起食物；更讓這對男女羨慕螞蟻擁有這麼多的家人和朋友，不像他們，只有兩個人相依為命。只有兩個人，真的是太寂寞了。

可是，要怎樣才能繁衍出自己的下一代作伴呢？他們感到困惑，不知道該怎麼辦？

為了可以生出下一代，這對男女嘗試了各種方式：從耳洞裡可不可以生出孩子？從嘴裡、從眼睛，還是從鼻子，行嗎？

可惜，這些方法都不成功。

女子回想起，當初自己破石而出的時候，曾經感覺到一陣怡人的輕風拂過巨石。

於是，女子特地爬上美麗的山峰，坐在山巔上將兩腿張開，讓風兒輕輕吹過全身，希望這種方式可以產生下一代。

可是，這個方法也失敗了，她還是沒有生出小孩。

兩個人為了繁衍的問題，越來越煩惱。

有一天，當他們正在休息時，看見蒼蠅飛來飛去。忽然，一對正在進行交配的蒼蠅，彼此相疊的停在地面上。

兩人恍然大悟，原來這就是繁衍後代的方法啊！

有了蒼蠅的啟示，他們心中產生默契。為了擁有自己的下一代，為了讓人類繁衍，此時，應該是兩人成親的時候了。

可是，男子覺得自己和女子一起從巨石生出來，又共同生活了那麼久，情同兄妹啊！所以，他始終害羞而不敢跟女子成親。

女子了解男子的心思，但她知道繁衍後代對人類來說，是非常神聖、重要的事情；而且，她心中也非常渴望擁有自己的孩子，就像所有的動物的媽媽一樣。

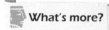

What's more?

住處：傳統的泰雅族人住在竹屋裡，竹屋的樑柱用櫸木、檜木為材，屋頂和牆用桂竹築成。沒有桂竹的地方，就把木柴劈成片狀圍成牆，屋頂則使用檜木皮。

於是，她決心想辦法幫助男子除去心中的障礙，與自己成親。

這一天，男子清晨醒來的時候，發現身邊的女子突然不知去向，這是從來沒有發生過的事啊！他急得四處尋找，並且發狂地跑遍了一座又一座的山，但都沒有發現女子的蹤影，他感到焦慮又傷心。

有天傍晚，男子奔走了一整天還是找不到女子，失望地走回住處。突然，在溪邊的大樹後面，看見有個人影一閃而過。

男子機警的跑過去，一下子就把那人給逮住了，他仔細一看，是個女人呢！

男子喜出望外，以為是他的女伴。然而，這女人的臉龐黝黑，從來就沒有見過。

男子雖然失望，但一個人的日子畢竟太寂寞，現在有了新同伴，自然感到相當開心，於是他將女子帶回住處。當天晚上，兩人順利地成了親。

第二天清晨，男子從香甜的夢中醒來，撞見女子正在洗臉，當她轉過頭來，哇！竟然就是他朝思暮想的女伴啊！男子內心既興奮、又感動。

原來，聰明的女子知道男子害羞，不敢跟自己成親，於是離開他，找煤炭把臉頰塗黑，偽裝成另外一名女子，再回到住處，跟男子成親。

過了一段時間，女子終於產下了自己的第一個孩子，兩人也完成了繁衍後代的任務。這就是當今泰雅族的起源。

What's more?

把臉頰給塗黑：故事中的女子把臉頰塗黑，流傳為泰雅族後來的紋面習俗。泰雅語稱紋面為瑪大斯(matas)。

02

神奇的呼喚術

以前泰雅族人生活上所需的山豬野味、山泉、木柴、小米等，只要呼喚就有，不必辛苦的耕作、打獵、挑水、砍柴。但是，人類太貪心，辜負了大自然的賜與，現在都要用勞力才能換取溫飽。

泰雅族的祖先在古時候，曾有一段自在、幸福的日子。

當時，生活非常輕鬆愉快，根本不需要像現在這樣辛苦賣力地耕作、打獵，就可以過著衣食無缺的日子。

那時候，所有的生活必需品，都是按照人們的需要，只要呼喚幾聲，就可以得到。

比如說，如果有人想吃山豬肉，只要發出「發呵！發呵！發呵！」的呼喚，山豬就會自動跑來。

更神奇的是，只要拔下山豬身上的幾根毛，然後用竹簍將豬毛蓋起來，等待片刻之後，掀開竹簍蓋子，豬毛就會變成鮮美的山豬肉，可以拿來下鍋煮食，大快朵頤一番了。

其他的獸肉、魚蝦以及蜂蜜、果實……，也都可以用這種呼喚的方式取得。

用來清洗食物、器皿或拿來飲用的山泉水，只要呼喊：「葛夏～葛夏～」，廚房裡的大水缸就會注滿清水。

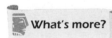

What's more?

耕作(pqumah，抹苟傌哈)：泰雅族人依環境及氣候的特性，發展出先進而環保的「耨耕」，它的特徵是淺耕，手握小鍬除草、種植作物，多為女性從事。另外還有「燒墾」的耕作方式，叫做mnayang抹哪樣，用火燒雜木叢生的山坡之後，灰燼可當天然肥料。

山豬(bzyok qnhyun，簸右葛呢迅)：而泰雅族人呼喊山豬的聲音為「發呵」(vha)。

竹簍(yawa，亞娃)：，用竹片編成的簍子，用來裝甘藷、芋頭之類的容器。

葛夏(qsya)：泰雅族人呼喊山泉水的聲音，在泰雅語指的是水。

所以，當時的泰雅族人都不必上山打獵，也不用下河捕魚，更不必辛苦地到溪邊汲水，就可以煮出各種美食了。

米飯又是怎麼來的呢？當然也很簡單。當時泰雅族人雖然也有農忙的時候，不過，比起現在的農夫，可就輕鬆多了。

所謂的農忙，也不過只是照顧自己家所種的一株稻子或小米，每天只要好好灌溉它，等它長大結穗，一串稻穗便足以讓一家人整整一年吃得飽。

煮飯時，只要取一粒放入鍋裡，也不用費心洗米，煮熟時就會變成一大鍋香噴噴、熱騰騰的米飯，足夠全家吃飽。

如果要出遠門，只要將米粒裝在耳管內，就可以提供許多天的需要。

那麼，煮飯時燃燒用的木柴又是如何取得的呢？當然也是靠呼喚而來啊！只要呼喚木柴：「葛侯盾！葛侯盾！」

木柴就會爭先恐後的由大門、窗戶走進來，自動跑到爐灶旁邊排排站，等著主人去燃火烹煮。

這麼幸運的不必為生活拼命辛苦工作，當時泰雅族人的祖先對於這些呼之即來的物品，抱著感恩與珍惜的態度，絕不會做出浪費的行為。因此，泰雅族祖先們度過了許多年快樂的生活。

What's more?

農忙：通常指作物播種、收割的時候。泰雅族主要的作物是陸稻、小米、黍、甘藷，也栽種樹豆、花生、薑、菜、芭蕉、苧麻、蓪草及煙草。

耳管(qengay，給奈)：泰雅族人為了增加美觀，在七、八歲左右，會在耳垂穿洞，並以茅草莖穿入，隨時日而增加草莖的數量，直到可以嵌入竹管為止，穿耳多半選在酷寒的冬天施行。

葛侯盾(qhunig)：泰雅族人呼喊的木柴聲音，在泰雅語指的是木柴。

不過，快樂的日子沒有維持很久。

有一天，有個婦人在「發呵！發呵！發呵！」呼喚山豬的時候，心中興起了貪念。

婦人心想：「每次拔了豬毛煮出來的肉都不是很多，只是剛好吃飽，實在不過癮。如果直接切下豬肉，看看會不會煮出更多？」

她正在想壞主意的時候，山豬跑來了，那婦人拿出刀子，毫不猶豫地一下子就把山豬的耳朵給切了下來。

山豬痛得「悠克～悠克～悠克～」邊叫邊跑開，逃入深山裡去了。」

山豬告訴其他動物牠淒慘的遭遇，一隻年邁的野鹿王聽了山豬的敘述，含著眼淚說：「啊！我們動物憐憫人類的辛勞，用真心誠意提供他們的需要。沒想到他們竟然如此殘忍，忘恩負義。哼！從此以後，我們沒有必要再幫助人類了。」

於是，所有的動物再也不應人類的呼喚而出現。人類如果想要吃鮮美的野味，必須靠自己翻山越嶺，上山打獵，甚至與雄壯的大熊、山豬搏鬥，打贏了才可以取得美味。

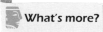

What's more?

悠克(ywak)：泰雅族人形容山豬疼痛的叫聲。

鍋子(kluban，葛魯半)：過去沒有鍋子的時代，泰雅族祖先使用燒烤的方式煮食。傳統的烹煮器具有大梧桐樹挖空製作的蒸桶、陶鍋等。

沒有了豐美的肉食，至少還有香噴噴的米飯吧！

然而，有一個女人因為偷懶也把稻米給得罪了。懶女人心想，「每次這樣煮一粒米才能吃一餐，實在麻煩，如果能一次煮一大把米，應該可以好幾天都不用煮飯了，這樣不是很輕鬆嗎？」

懶女人便抓了一大把米下鍋去煮，米飯滾開時，鍋蓋被撐得像要爆炸似的。

懶女人掀開鍋蓋一瞧，哇！不得了！整鍋的米飯霎時變成一隻隻的鳥兒，由鍋裡「巴爾！巴爾！巴爾！」地往外衝出去了……

懶女人驚訝地張口結舌，看著鳥兒往屋外飛去，並且聽到鳥兒七嘴八舌地說著：「懶惰的人啊！懶惰的人啊！從此以後，你們不再擁有輕鬆的日子囉！如果想得到溫飽，就必須開墾土地，辛勤地在田裡揮汗耕作，才能有收穫。」

她還聽見一些鳥兒嘰嘰喳喳的笑著說：「我們會在你們收割稻米之前，飛到田裡去吃你們的稻穀喔！你們最好勤勞一點，好好的看顧那些稻田，免得被我們吃光喔！」

鳥兒邊說邊向窗外的樹林飛去。

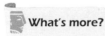 **What's more?**

開墾土地(mnayang，抹哪樣)：泰雅族領域多為大坡度的高山地形，使用特有的「燒墾」方式開墾土地。種植約兩三年，就在該地種植赤楊木休耕，讓土地休息，轉往他處開墾。

鳥兒(pzit，波記特)：就是麻雀的意思。

但是，噩運到此還沒有結束。

有個年輕男子又惹禍了。這個年輕男子不肯努力工作，整天喜歡捉弄人，尤其常常挑逗女生，是個很不受歡迎的人。

有一天，年輕人走在山路上，卻正好看見一排木柴「咚！咚！咚！」，正準備進入某一人家的廚房去。

年輕人又想要惡作劇了，躲進路旁草叢，等到木柴走到身旁，冷不防跳出草叢「哇～～～」的大吼一聲，嚇得整排木柴立刻四散奔逃，躲入叢林裡。木柴禁不起這麼驚嚇，再也不敢靠近人類了。

當然，從此以後人們若要生火燒烤，都必須到深山裡砍柴，並且得靠自己的力氣挑柴囉！

由於人類辜負大自然的賜與，山豬、野鹿、山泉、木柴、小米等不再信任人類。從此以後泰雅族人就要辛苦的耕作、打獵、挑水、砍柴……，用勞力換取溫飽。

泰雅族的祖先因而不時告誡後代子孫：「不可浪費」、「不可貪心」、「不可懶惰」、「不可惡作劇」，這樣的態度不單是對人，對於土地、大自然也是一樣的。

03

彩虹橋的審判

每個泰雅族人死後的的靈魂,都要通過往靈界的美麗彩虹橋,接受它的審判。勇敢、正直、遵守「嘎嘎」的人,便可以在祖靈歡迎下順利走過去。

雨過天晴，橫跨天際的美麗彩虹，總是令人驚嘆。然而，彩虹在泰雅族人的眼中，具有神聖莊嚴的意義。

大人們會告誡孩子：「千萬不要用手去指神靈之橋，這樣會觸犯禁忌。」

彩虹在泰雅族人的傳說中，是一條通往靈界的橋，具有審理與判決人間善惡曲直的能力。

傳說中，神靈之橋是一位名叫卜大的人幻化而來的。

據說卜大長相孔武威猛，力大無窮，可以徒手與黑熊搏鬥。他不但是個勇敢的獵人，平日也按照「嘎嘎」待人處世。泰雅族人除了佩服他的勇氣，也尊重他的人格，所以卜大自然而然地成為泰雅族裡的精神領袖。

卜大富有正義感，處事公正，族人有任何糾紛或爭議，都會請他協調裁決。遇到冥頑不靈的人，卜大只要怒吼一聲，那人就會嚇得當場渾身發抖，不敢再囂張。

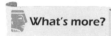

What's more?

彩虹(hongu utux，吼怒・巫渡)：也就是神靈之橋的意思。泰雅族人相信人死後，靈魂都要到永恆的靈界與死去的祖靈相聚。從人間通往靈界是一條漫漫遙遠的路程。在靈界的入口處，架有彎弓似的美麗彩虹橋，是死去的靈魂必經的地方。

觸犯禁忌(psaniq，伯撒呢呀)：包括一般生活上的(例如男女的分際、狩獵的禁忌)、祭典儀式上的(例如祭典前不與外人接觸)所有必須注意，且嚴禁觸犯的規條，以免去觸怒神靈，招致個人以及族群的不幸。

靈界('tuxan，厄篤翰)：神靈之所在地。

卜大(buta)：當卜大死後，名字前面加上gun的接頭語，稱為耿卜大(gun・buta)，以表示對過世的人的尊重。泰雅族人深信偉人耿卜大的魂魄變成了高掛在天際的彩虹，不論男女老少，死後都必須經過這座彩虹橋的審判。

每年到了狩獵、播種、收割、祭祖等儀式進行時，族人也會請示卜大的意見。

當然，卜大也全心全力為族人服務，他愛護族人，恩威並施，泰雅族人敬他如神。

當卜大年邁，知道自己將不久於人世，便交代族人說：「我死後，將化成彩虹，高掛在天邊，護祐子孫。你們要記住祖先的嘎嘎，不可以任意違背……」說完，隨即閉上眼睛離開人世。

當他去世時，天際果然出現一道美麗弧形的彩虹。耿卜大成了通往靈界的橋樑，他以泰雅祖先的「嘎嘎」，審視、評斷所有的死者。

根據泰雅的古訓，男子要獵取山豬、山鹿、黑熊等大型野獸，甚至要出草砍取敵人的首級，努力使自己成為一個勇敢善獵的人。

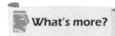

What's more?

嘎嘎(gaga，嘎嘎)：是一切風俗習慣嘎嘎 及生活規範的統稱，以及族人共同遵循的習俗和文化信仰。「嘎嘎」有多種涵意，也可以是族人的一種互助團體的稱呼，相同的團體會共同制定是非善惡標準，一起舉行祭典儀式，在開墾、播種、收割，或建屋等工作繁忙的時候，也相互支援。所以，「嘎嘎」是泰雅社會結合的重要因素，也是泰雅族人的生活重心。

精神領袖(mrhuw，模勒互)：泰雅族沒有貴族或階級制度，部落中年長、勇敢、有智慧、公平正義的人，就是部落的「精神領袖」。精神領袖不是父傳子的世襲制，與頭目或貴族制度不同。

出草(mgaga，抹嘎嘎)：其中加m (抹)使gaga轉成動詞，有「執行」的意思。而嘎嘎(gaga)指泰雅族一切規範、法律、祭儀的總稱，mgaga 就是去執行祖先傳統的規範。所以，古時候泰雅族人出草獵敵首，是執行一項神聖的儀式。

女人則要熟習抽麻捻紗的織布技巧，勤於山田種植，讓自己成為勤勞能幹的女人。

如果男子在生前謹守「嘎嘎」，驍勇善獵，那麼在他死後，這些被他獵殺的動物與敵人的亡魂，將會簇擁著男子的靈，一路浩浩蕩蕩的前往靈界。

當如此壯觀的隊伍來到靈界時，去世的祖靈也會以同樣的陣勢出來相迎，讓這名男子，不但可以在去世後無愧的面對祖靈，更會感到無比的驕傲和風光。

相反的，若是膽小笨拙、輕浮懶惰的人，死後只能落魄寂寥地一個人走上通往靈界的道路，而且不會有祖靈出來迎接。

在前往靈界的入口，還有耿卜大幻化的神靈之橋把關，靈橋下是萬丈深淵，住著無數飢餓的毒蛇巨蟒和兇猛的鱷魚。

勇敢正直的人，可以堂堂正正安然通過這座橋，順利到達靈界。生性膽小、懶怠的人，死後看見高掛天際的靈橋，心生慚愧，多半會繞道而行。不過，繞行的道路是遙遠坎坷、荊棘叢生，這些沒辦法通過考驗的靈魂，只好在荒郊野外遊蕩，永遠到不了靈界。

不遵守「嘎嘎」的規範，做惡多端的人，死後在靈橋前，如果仍不知檢討自己的惡行，硬要走過去；那麼，當他走到橋中間，靈橋便會自動翻轉，闖關的靈魂便跌落萬丈深淵，成為巨蟒、鱷魚的食物。

所以，每當彩虹出現的時候，通常會伴隨隆隆的雷聲，泰雅族人便認為那是耿卜大雄偉的吼聲，時時提醒著：「不可以過著頑劣、胡亂的日子，必須遵守祖先傳下來的『嘎嘎』，規規矩矩的生活。」

部落百寶盒 ｜｜ 傳授哈「原」秘笈，搖身變成泰雅通

一、泰雅族的生命禮俗

▶ 多子多孫壯大族群

一般來說，泰雅族人希望子女眾多，對於新生兒的誕生都非常歡欣，因為在泰雅族的社會中，認為強盛的族群，並不在於廣大的土地或豐富的財產，而在於眾多的壯丁。

▶ 祓除不淨迎接新生

傳說中，泰雅族的社會有重視男子的傾向，主要是因為婚嫁時，女子要嫁到男方家。但在父母撫育子女的態度上，並不會因此而輕視女兒，對待男孩女孩都是一樣的。

不過，傳統的泰雅族人認為分娩是不乾淨的，必須進行祓除儀式。這個儀式由部落中的女巫以燃燒樟木片同時唸咒的方式進行，並且祈福。有些是產婦或家人自己進行祓除儀式，但須在離家稍遠的地方，替新生兒祈福。同時產婦家要釀酒、宰豬招待親族朋友。而被招待的族人也以衣物、珠飾、酒肉等送給產婦家，慶祝生子。

依照泰雅族傳統的習俗，產婦在生產完一年之內或嬰兒滿月時，要與丈夫一起帶著新生的嬰兒和禮物（山豬肉、醃肉、小米糕等）回娘家報喜，並且在娘家住上幾天。女方家族傍晚會在院子燃起篝火，將這些食物拿出來給部落的親友分享，並且飲酒作樂，慶祝一番。

▶ 命名不忘父祖輩

新生兒誕生之後，父母會請家裡的長輩，或族裡的長老幫孩子取名字。泰雅族沒有表示家族的姓氏，只有表示個人的名字，命名方式是採用父子（女）

聯名的方式，就是在自己的名字後面加上父親的名字。例如：「馬紹·阿紀」，就是指「馬紹」這個人，而「阿紀」是馬紹的爸爸。千萬不要叫他「馬先生」或「阿紀先生」喔！直接稱他「馬紹」就對了。

如果兩個同名的人在一起，或提起兩個同名的人時，就會加上各自的父親名字作為區別。如果正好兩位的父親又同名，就再加上祖父的名字作為區分，這樣的區別可以數上一長串哩！

泰雅族通常沿用古代傳下來的姓名，一聽就知道是男子或女子。例如：尤浩、尤命、婁幸、以範…等是男子名。雅外、里夢、瓦夏、比黛、里慕依、撒韻…等是女子名字。當然，也有許多名字是採用動植物、日常器具、自然現象或抽象名詞而來的。

▶ 成年的記號

在傳統的泰雅族社會中，男女青年到了大約十四、五歲左右，就要施行「紋面」的成年禮儀式。紋面就是在臉上刺青，男子必須通過「驍勇善獵」（曾經獵取敵人首級或大型獵物者）的考驗，女子必須是「心細手巧」（善於織布、懂種植作物、打理家務）的人，才有資格紋面，也才算是真正成年的人。所以，紋面可以說是泰雅族男女「成年」的象徵。

▶ 婚姻大事按部就班

傳統的泰雅族認為，青年在舉行過成年禮之後，才成為真正的男人和女人，也才可以開始談論婚嫁。如果沒有經過成年禮就開始結交異性朋友，據說他的家人會遭受到神的處罰。

當一個成年男子向家長及部落長老表明他喜歡某一位女子時，長老會派代表前往查詢那位女子是否成年，如果是，那麼男方會選擇一個日子，由部落長老和家族代表為該男子前往求親。如果女方家長同意，他們會請家族的女性長輩告訴那位女子這樁求婚的事。如果女子也同意，這個親事就算成功，這對男女就可以準備結婚了。

▶ 以胎兒姿勢告別人世的蹲距葬

過去泰雅族人的喪葬很特別，當一個人過世的時候，就在死者的床下掘一個墓穴，並且是深而窄的「豎坑」。

親人會幫過世的人梳洗換裝，並且佩戴耳飾、首飾、手環、臂飾、胸兜等服飾，盛裝打扮一番。然後將死者調整成蹲距的姿勢，也就是雙腳彎曲到腹部，雙手環抱胸前，恰如胎兒在母親子宮裡的姿勢。然後用方形的麻布把屍首擺在中央，四角拉起包裹好，在頭頂的上方打結，再將屍首以及死者日常所用的物品安置於墓穴中，上方覆以石板，再填上厚土。

為過世的親友哀傷，是人之常情不分種族的，傳統泰雅族的喪葬除了墓穴為特別的「豎坑」以及屍首的「蹲距葬」之外，喪禮期間也不歡樂、少與外界往來、不參加祭典等等。然而，泰雅人採用如胎兒蹲距的姿勢告別人世，感覺上像是回歸大地母親的懷抱，這在視土地、大自然為生命的泰雅族人來說，應該是最能讓死者感到安慰的。

二、不可失傳的傳統技藝

▶ 織布是泰雅婦女的榮耀

泰雅族的織布技巧，是台灣原住民當中的佼佼者，也是泰雅女子的榮耀。織布的材料以苧麻為主，族人自己栽種苧麻，採收後紡成麻線，織成麻布，用來做衣服。

在泰雅族紡織布紋的設計上，可以發現許多優美的花紋和圖案，而衣物常以白色貝珠來綴飾，稱為珠衣或貝衣。 麻線的製作過程極為繁瑣，首先將成熟苧麻砍下，用竹製刮器將苧麻皮刮成纖維抽出麻絲，再把麻絲製成麻線。麻線必須清洗、擰乾，再摻和米糠粉末使它柔軟，再混合炭灰水煮約三小時，使之軟線並漂白，接著以清水洗淨披掛在戶外，接受曝曬雨淋，越久顏色顯得越白。

織布時將白線條理成環型置於木架上配色，所呈現的線條有一定的圖形，而且以幾何形狀為主，如三角形、菱形、直橫紋、斜紋、波紋等，加上強烈的顏色對比，給人鮮明活潑的感覺。

泰雅族女子在很小的時候就要開始學習製作麻紗、紡線，年紀稍大時開始學習用整經機整經理線，接著再學習用織布機織布。泰雅族服飾上的花紋圖案，是經緯線上架時，利用不同顏色的經線以數個梭子挑起來，再穿入緯線，浮織出多樣的花紋，這個動作非常繁複，通常由女兒坐在母親身旁，日復一日觀看仿效而學得的。

▶ 日常編織才能不可少

另外，「竹編」與「籐編」是泰雅族的兩種重要的編織材料。竹編，顧名思義就是用竹片編織，而籐編則是用籐編織的器具。桂竹是泰雅族人常用的主要建材，也是編織最好的材料之一。

以竹片編織成的器具有大篩子、小篩子、竹簍、魚籃、雞籃。而籐，有柔軟強韌不易斷裂的特性，所以也很適合編成各種器具，如帽子、籐包、背籃、條帶等，精緻而實用。

三、紋面文化與文飾

▶ 紋面的由來

泰雅族紋面的習俗歷史悠久，真正的由來已不可考。有一種說法認為，紋面是泰雅族祖先為了讓下一代有過人的膽識而設定的一個標識。也有一說認為，紋面是一種辨識作用，平時以紋面作為同族人的標誌，在與敵人作戰時可以辨識自己人，以免誤殺。

此外，過世的泰雅族人以紋面與否來判別是不是可以順利通過靈界的「彩虹橋」，到達祖靈的所在。在泰雅族起源「巨石生人」的神話傳說中，女子將臉頰塗黑，以便與情同手足的男子成親，並繁衍後代。於是紋面成為後人判定年輕男女是否可以成婚的標準。

▶ 紋面象徵著美麗與榮耀

當然，紋面在傳統的泰雅族社會，不僅只是屆齡成婚的標誌，那也是美觀的標準，更是榮耀的象徵。

最普遍的紋面圖案，是男子在額頭中央一豎，下巴中央一豎；女子則是在額頭中央一豎，和以嘴唇四周為起點，沿著臉頰兩邊往上彎到耳際為止，像彩虹弧形一樣的圖案。

▶ 裝飾品的各種面貌

泰雅族人在衣服之外，還有各種佩戴在身上的裝飾品。主要有頭環、頸飾、胸飾、臂飾、耳飾（或耳管）、手環、指環、腳飾等等。

這些裝飾品都是自製的，其中有男女都可佩戴的、有男性或女性專用的；有任何人都可以佩戴的、有須具有某種資格才可以佩戴的。

例如臂環，是只有男子才可以佩戴的，每個男子都可以佩戴一個在左臂或右臂，但是若非曾經斬獲敵首的男子，不得兩手同時佩戴。不曾獵獲野豬等大型獵物的男子，則不得佩戴豬牙作成的臂飾。

手環，是男女都可以佩戴的，但若不是已獵取敵首的男子，或不是擅長織布的女子，就不得雙手佩戴。

四、英雄戰鬥與出草傳說

泰雅族人狩獵的方式大約分成兩種，一種是「追獵」，就是將野獸追到很近的距離時，再用獵刀刺擊或長槍射擊，使野獸受傷倒地，然後捕捉回家；另一種是「守獵」，也就是觀察野獸經常出沒的路徑，然後在適當的地點埋設陷阱，使野獸誤踩陷阱，無法逃脫，予以捕捉。

▶「頭目」的階級制度不存在

在泰雅族社會體制中，並沒有所謂的「頭目」。雖然在族裡面有巫師、熊人（指英勇的人）、紋面師、嫻熟深奧語言等等受族人尊敬的人，但那些都不是屬於階級性的職位，純粹只是他們自己技藝方面的專長，而由別人給予的封號而已。

泰雅族人的性格先天好強、自我意識非常強烈，在誰也不願屈居人下的心態之下，常演變成各自為首的社會局面，所以並沒有發展成類似他族「頭目」的階級制度。

不過，在泰雅族社會裡，卻有一種人被稱為麼勒戶（mrhuw），就是在言行舉止、智慧、技藝各方面表現出眾又穩重的人，每當族裡發生自己無法解決的事情，就會邀請mrhu協助解決或做決定。

然而，mrhu的生活和一般族人沒有兩樣，沒有奉給也沒有稅收。住屋或服飾也都和族人相同，他一樣作農、一樣狩獵，所不同的是他比一般族人更冷靜、穩重、有智慧、有口才，受到族人特別的敬重，因而通常可以代表族人對外發表意見，是精神上及意見上的領袖。 出草是執行祖先傳下的儀式 泰雅族稱「出草」為抹嘎嘎（mgaga），嘎嘎（gaga）指泰雅族一切規範、法律、祭儀的總稱，mgaga 就是去執行祖先傳統的規範，其中加m (抹)使gaga轉成動詞，有「執行」的意思。所以，古時候泰雅族人出草獵敵首，是執行一項神聖的儀式。

出草，就是到部落以外獵取敵人首級的行為。出草與戰鬥不同的是，它的目的只在獵取敵人的首級，並不是為了消滅敵人的勢力，雖然出草時也掠取敵人的財物，但這不是出草主要的目的。而出草主要的目的大致有三點：

▶ 出草的目的之一、為了決定爭議的曲直

如果族裡發生不能解決的爭議時，雙方就分別出草，仰賴神靈的審判，決定誰是誰非。因為泰雅族人認為神靈必定會幫助有理的一方，在出草的時候保佑其順利獵取首級。如果雙方都取得首級，或都沒有取得首級，就再出草一次，直到有一方屈服為止。

當出草的勝敗還沒有決定之前，爭執的雙方族人處於敵對的關係，不互相往來、路上見面也不互相交談，並且雙方不能一起狩獵、耕作，這在互助的泰雅族來說是很不方便的，所以經常會有一方持續不下去而向另一方屈服。

因為自己族人雙方爭執，卻去獵取他族的首級，聽起來實在不是理性的行為。可是這一點泰雅族有個說法，說這個行為是基於古代泰雅族祖先與他族（被獵者）祖先所締結的契約，所以泰雅族才稱「出草」為mgaga，有「執行祖先傳下來之正當權力」之意。（訂定契約的過程，在泰雅族神話傳說中是有典故的，在此略過。）

▶ 出草的目的之二、為近親報仇

泰雅族人若是被人殺害，被害人的父子、兄弟、堂（表）兄弟等近親有為他報仇的義務。加害者如果是自己的族人，就以贖物的方式贖罪來解決。如果是他族或雖為同族人，卻正處於敵對狀態的時候，就必須出草報仇。不過，不一定要殺害加害者本人，只要獵取加害者部落族人任何一人就可以了。

▶ 出草的目的之三、為了得到男子勇武之表彰

在泰雅族裡，一個男子必須勇武，這是面對異族以及敵族維持自己族人生存所必要的資格。因此，一個男子近成年卻從未獵取首級的人，被認為不是真正的男人，也沒資格紋面。相反的，若能獵取首級，除了可以紋面之外，還可以佩戴象徵榮耀的飾品，在部落裡受人敬重。

不過，光為表彰勇武而出草的比例不多，出草原因多為解決爭執以及報仇者。

出草的方式從準備、啟程、襲擊、凱旋、到招魂都有嚴謹的規矩與禁忌必須遵守。所以，出草在傳統的泰雅族人心目中，是非常莊嚴神聖與重要的一種儀式。當然，這個習俗在現今泰雅族社會早已絕跡，大家不必心生恐懼。

五、泰雅族的食物

近代以來，目前泰雅族人主要糧食的取得大多靠農耕栽種，少部分靠採集野生植物。至於肉類則為狩獵、捕魚、採蜂，族人也豢養家禽家畜。

▶ 自給自足的飲食態度

泰雅族日常烹煮食物，多半以蒸煮、火烤的方式進行，菜蔬多為水煮。肉類則會以燒烤及用鹽醃漬來處理。烹煮食物的器具有陶、罐、竹筒、木製蒸桶、青銅鍋、錫鍋。

泰雅族人在開墾新地時，是採用火耕的方式，也就是將土地上的雜木草叢用火燒淨，燃燒剩下的灰燼當成土地的養分，然後整地播種耕種。泰雅族人對土地的執著是無與倫比的，土地濫墾、森林濫伐都是被禁止的。而耕種面積以自給自足為度。

▶ 尊重自然，與土地相依存

農忙時族人都互相支援，以便調配勞力。耕地在耕作三、四年後，就遷往別處開墾新地，舊地就種植赤楊木，暫時放置不用，等待地力自然恢復，以備他日之用。自古以來，泰雅族人即遵循大自然法則，與土地相依相存，如此維續族群與土地的生命。

▶ 泰雅族主要糧食一覽表

穀　類	稻米、栗、黍（小米）、高粱等
塊根類	蕃薯、芋頭、淮山、山藥等
豆　類	樹豆、長豆、毛豆、豌豆、綠豆、花生等
瓜　類	黃瓜、絲瓜、南瓜、胡瓜等
蔬菜類	小白菜、藤心、鵝菜、以及野生的山萵苣、龍葵等
肉　類	家畜、家禽、野獸類、魚類、蜂類等等
水　果	香蕉、桃子、櫻桃、李子、枇杷、梅子、鳳梨、柿子、百香果、甘蔗、等等
配料與辛香料	山胡椒、茱萸、香菜、生薑、香菇、木耳、各種野菇

六、泰雅族的祖靈祭

泰雅族最早的祖先生活在高山叢林中，以狩獵、種植、採集的方式取得糧食。因此，泰雅族人對於「大自然」這個提供生存所需的生活環境，抱著極為慎重與敬畏的態度。

在泰雅族的社會中，有關狩獵、種植的運作，都必須配合自然環境的變化，以及祖先傳下來的生活智慧，訂有嚴密的嘎嘎（gaga），並發展出泰雅族特有的祝福、祈求，以及感恩的祭儀。

▶ 祭儀中須遵守戒律和禁忌

每年新曆的六、七月間，會舉行一個很重要的祭典儀式，叫做「斯密悠思」（smyus），也就是祖靈祭。在祖靈祭之前，男人要上山打獵，女人釀酒，以備祭儀之用；族人必須遵守「抹匠」（mijil），也就是要守戒律、不可觸犯禁忌，像是在祖靈祭舉行的前一天下午，就要進行「換火」，就是把爐灶的餘灰清除乾淨，重新燃火，那火一直要維持燃燒狀態，到祭典結束以前不能熄滅。這時後也禁止觸摸生麻、禁用裁縫織布的麻線，也不可使用針、剪刀、小刀等。

「抹匠」（mijil）時間更要保持與外界隔絕，不可以和外界往來，親友暫時不互相拜訪。若是在舉行祖靈祭時，不巧有遠道而來且不便返回的親友，那麼主人會在離家不遠處搭建一座竹製的臨時屋，讓親友暫住。換句話說，泰雅族的祖靈祭具有秘密性，屬於個別家族的祭儀，不能讓外人隨便參與。

在祖靈祭的前夕，戶長會率領家中男子到屋外不遠處呼喊：「所有過世的祖父輩、祖母輩、男長輩、女長輩…，明天凌晨我們相約在…。」與祖靈約定隔天凌晨祖靈祭的地點，懇請祖靈到時一定要依約前來。

晚上，家人就把當季收穫的穀物（玉米、粟米、稻米）製成「黑葛印」（hekil），也就是黏糕，並將狩獵所捕獲的獸肉，煮熟後各以「李桁」（li-hang，學名山芙蓉）的葉子包裹，用細麻繩捆綁好，每個大約像帶殼花生般的大小。然後，再將新釀的酒裝在竹筒裡，以備第二天祖靈祭之用。

▶ 以肅穆且虔誠的心祭拜祖靈

泰雅族人祭拜祖靈（utux，巫渡呼），的供品不需要太大，因為泰雅族人認為祖靈具有著神奇力量，只需聞到氣味就可以飽足。

到達約定的地點，就把酒食祭品分別綁在樹枝上，由家長祈福之後，所有成員大聲呼喊，邀請各代祖靈，以及逝去的親人攜手前來享用祭品。

直到天快要亮時，所有人就回家去，離開時不可以轉頭去看舉行祭典的地方，樹上的祭品就讓它自然消失，不必再拿下來。回到家後，家族共同享用所有酒食、獸肉歡慶豐收。

祖靈祭是泰雅族人一年中很重要的祭儀之一，直到現在，還保持這個祭祖的儀式。從祭儀的過程，可以看出泰雅族人對於祖靈庇佑收穫的感恩，是謹慎恭謹、虔誠而內斂的。這也正是泰雅族祖先生活在叢山峻嶺中，辛苦取得糧食的過程，而所發展出的生活態度，也代代相傳直到如今。

造訪部落　**部落藏寶圖，來挖泰雅寶**

看過了泰雅族的神話與傳說故事，知道了泰雅族祖先如何繁衍自己的後代；卜大如何懲處不遵守嘎嘎的死後靈魂；以及過去泰雅族人曾有多麼美好的時光，是否仍覺得意猶未盡呢！

泰雅族是台灣第二大的原住民族，人口總數約九萬餘人（註一），佔整個原住民人口的百分之二十三。分布在台北縣、宜蘭縣、桃園縣、新竹縣、苗栗縣、台中縣、南投縣、花蓮縣及高雄縣少數地區。現在，透過這份精心編製的「泰雅族部落導覽圖」，陪伴身歷其境，盡情挖掘部落文化寶藏，保證不虛此行。

當然，造訪部落時更不能錯過泰雅族豐富的祭儀活動，例如每年七月舉行的豐年祭。心動想要行動之前，可要記得先查詢確切時間及地點，建議上網站或聯絡各鄉鎮公所原住民行政課。

・台北縣政府原住民行政局02-29686898分機3612

・宜蘭縣政府原住民行政課03-9364567分機1241

・花蓮縣政府原住民輔導行政課03-8234531分機370

・新竹縣政府原住民行政課03-5518101分機246

・桃園縣政府原住民行政局03-3321101分機5611

・南投縣政府原住民行政局049-2243637

・苗栗縣政府原住民課037-322150分機341

・台中縣政府原住民行政課042-5263100分機2130

・高雄縣政府原住民局行政課07-7477611分機2105
　　註一：2002年12月原民會資料

泰雅族
文化導覽圖

族語開口說 **入境隨俗的泰雅語**

你好嗎？
Lokah su' ga?
婁嘎　素 ㄍㄚˇ？
好　　你

我很好　　　謝謝你
Lokah ku'.　mhuway su'
婁嘎　故　　麼懷　　素
好　　我　　謝謝　　妳

你叫什麼名字?
Ima' lalu su'?
以罵　喇路　素
誰　　名字　你

我叫瑁瑁·瑪邵
Meimei·Masow lalu'mu.
瑁瑁　·瑪邵　喇路 目
瑁瑁　·瑪邵　名字 我

你從哪裡來的？
Kahul su' inu'?
卡混　素　以怒
從　　你　哪裡

我來自鎮西堡
Kahul ku' Cinsbu'.
卡混　故　柬徒步
來自　我　鎮西堡

你是原住民嗎？
Tayel su'?
泰雅爾 素
原住民 你

是的
Aw.
阿物
是

你要去誰家？
Musa su ngasal ima?
牡薩　素　哪散　以罵
去　　你　家　　誰

我要去里慕伊的家
Musa saku ngsal Rimuy.
牡薩　撒故　哪撒　里慕伊
去　　我　　家　　里慕伊

再見了！
Sgaya　ta　la!
斯卡亞　達　辣
再見　　我們　了

族語開口說 泰雅族稱謂的介紹

yutas	猶大斯	祖父 外祖父 (爺爺輩的稱謂)
yaki'	雅紀	祖母 外祖母 (奶奶輩的稱謂)
yaba'	亞爸	爸爸
yaya'	亞軋	媽媽
mama'	馬罵	伯伯 叔叔 舅舅 姑丈
yata'	亞大	伯母 嬸嬸 阿姨 姑姑
qsuyan mlikuy	葛署宴 麼里故伊	哥哥
qsuyan kneril	葛署宴 葛餒蘭	姊姊
sswe' mlikuy	捨歲 麼里故伊	弟弟
sswe' kneril	捨歲 葛餒蘭	妹妹

學習加油站　本書漢語與泰雅語名詞對照表

故事01：巨石傳說

用漢字拼讀	泰雅語	漢語名詞
抹厄部 勒給亞	b'bu rgyax	山巔
葛拉乎 那 巴篤怒乎	krahu na btunux	巨石
賽斯巴幹	pinsebugan	分裂、裂開
抹里固一	mlikuy	男人
葛捏吝	kneril	女人
波卡怒乎	bqanux	山鹿
谷類黑	quleh	魚
否隆	bolung	蝦
卡嘎恩	kagang	蟹
了拉嗎特	rramat	蔬果
葛葛洗怒	qqsinuw	野味（獸類）
葛葛亞怒呼	qqyanux	動物
葛合呢訝	qhniq	鳥
烏度乎	utux	精靈
葛打呵益	qtahiy	螞蟻
古度乎 那散	qutux ngasal	家人
拉匿	rangi	朋友
拉給	laqiy	孩子
巴巴克	babak	耳朵（洞）
呢掛葛	ngqwaq	嘴巴
簍加葛	roziq	眼睛
努戶	nguhuw	鼻子
亞鬧烏	yangauw	後代、子孫
艮把翰	kinbahan	人類
史考利克	squliq	成親
抹什棍	msqun	兄妹
得歲	tswe	媽媽
呀呀	yaya	煤炭

用漢字拼讀	泰雅語	漢語名詞
勒給斯	rqyas	臉龐
把尬呵	bagah	煤炭
瑪大斯	Matas	紋面

故事02：神奇的呼喚術

用漢字拼讀	泰雅語	漢語名詞
抹苟偶哈	pqumah	耕作
抹哪樣	mnayang	燒墾(開墾土地)
葛馬路潑	qmalup	打獵
簸右葛呢迅	bzyok qnhyun	山豬
亞娃	yawa	竹簍
呵紀映	hzing	蜂蜜
得耨不一	tnobuiy	廚房
得把尬	tbaqa	大水缸
葛夏	qsya	水
把蓋	pagay	稻子(或小米)
簸谷罵呵	pqumah	農夫
給奈	qengay	耳管
葛侯盾	ghunig	木柴
卜彥	puyen	爐灶
卜力	buli	刀子
哪路呼	ngrux	熊
抹給浪	mqilang	懶惰
葛魯半	kluban	鍋子
波記特	pzit	麻雀
撥亞幹 耿亞給黑	byaqan kinyaqeh	噩運
葛婀蔓 合啦呵蔚	k'man hlhuy	草叢
卜呢依呀葛	puniaq	火
得抹苟尼呀葛	tmqoniaq	砍柴

用漢字拼讀	泰雅語	漢語名詞
金簸哇難	cibownan	大自然
勒合彥	rhiyal	土地
葛印簸給散	kinbkisan	祖先

故事03：彩虹橋的審判

用漢字拼讀	泰雅語	漢語名詞
吼怒‧巫渡	hongu utux	彩虹(神靈橋)
伯撒呢呀	psaniq	觸犯禁忌
厄篤翰	'tuxan	靈界
模勒互	mrhuw	精神領袖
哪路呼	ngarux	黑熊
撥卡路頗	pqalup	獵人
嘎嘎	gaga	儀式
巫渡呼	utux	神
斯勒技	slqiy	弓
抹嘎嘎	mgaga	出草
抹努卡	mnuka	抽麻
的米嫩	tminun	織布
麼固	mqu	蛇
比比映	bibing	巨蟒

部落百寶盒：泰雅族的祖靈祭

用漢字拼讀	泰雅語	漢語名詞
斯密悠思	smyus	祖靈祭
抹匠	mijil	守戒律、不可觸犯禁忌
黑葛印	hekil	黏糕
李桁	lihang	山芙蓉

布農族
Bunun

▶ 小筆記 ▶

・美妙的八部合音pasibutbut。
・傳統生活領域在跨中部、東部與南部的1500公尺以上高山地區，因次腿部最健美。
・「木刻畫曆」是台灣原住民中唯一的文字表徵。

· 典型的父系社會。

· 金曲講歌手秀蘭瑪雅、王宏恩都是布農族的光榮。

故事導讀　月亮、百步蛇與人的約定

射日是大家熟悉的神話母題，原住民各族對此也都有繁簡不等的敘述版本。相較於漢民族的后羿神話，原住民的射日行動，並不強調或突顯主角的英雄行為，換句話說，戡天役物的人類中心主義，不是原住民射日神話所欲彰顯的目標或價值。各讓一步，彼此尊重，才是天人關係的理想狀態。被射瞎的太陽，成了月亮，日夜的變化改變了萬物生存的形式與節奏，因而有了與月亮的約定。

整個的故事既然不是以英雄為中心，射日就不應當是一項浪漫且單獨的行動。流傳在原住民的射日神話當中，父子相偕出征，似乎是共同的希望。顯示射日不是一個孤立的事件，父子相互的合作，以及信念和意志的通傳，才是完成任務的關鍵。

人與天的倫理同樣適用於人與萬物之間。善於織布的卡布斯，為了給自己深愛的丈夫比馬編織一套圖案特殊的服飾，向母百步蛇商借小百步蛇來模仿；之後，竟失信於母百步蛇，將小百步蛇給折騰死了。從此便引發了幾個世紀的人蛇大戰，雙方都死傷慘重。問題的解決，依然仰賴雙方各退一步：百步蛇同意將身上美麗的圖案交給布農族，做為正式服裝的圖樣；布農族人也改以嚴肅、尊重的態度對待百步蛇，並稱牠為「朋友」。

獵人的信仰基本上即遵循了上述的邏輯，貪婪、傲慢和對大自然力量的違逆，終將導致滅亡。

「布農之女阿朵兒」的故事，則涉及到人與人、族群與族群之間的衝突，這通常比人與天、人與自然的矛盾更難解決。故事中的主角阿朵兒表現了布農族傳統女性的忠貞、堅忍、機智與勇氣，不僅成功地將兒子迪樣帶回了家鄉，也造就了他做為部落領袖的所有人格特質。阿朵兒最後幻化成夜鶯離迪樣而去，事實上也樹立了布農族傳統婦女忠貞不二的典範。

Reader's Guide   The Moon, the Hundred Pace Snake and Man's Promise

Shooting the sun is a familiar mythological motif, and all indigenous peoples also have various narratives. Compared with the Han Chinese mythology of Hou-yi, these stories do not emphasize or highlight the heroic behavior of a protagonist. In other words, the anthropocentrism of conquering the heavens and enslavement of others, is far from the intent or purpose of these indigenous' sun-shooting stories. No, backing away and mutual respect is the ideal state of the relationship between heavens and humans. is to make concessions and respect each other. One of the suns, blinded by the archer's arrows became the moon, while the changes of day and night changed the form and rhythm, changed the very the existence of all beings and phenomena and led to an agreement with the moon.

There is no hero around which this story centers. Whereas many might think shooting the sun sounds like a romantic deed, this is far from the case. Indigenous sun-shooting stories show a common hope of the father and son as they embark on a common endeavor. The story shows that shooting the sun is not an isolated event. Key to accomplishing the task is the cooperation between father and son, as well as their communication of belief and will.

The ethics of human's relationship with the heavens also applies between humans and the myriad beings and phenomena. So, when Qabus, the talented weaver, in order to create special patterns for the clothes of her beloved husband, Bima, borrows a baby hundred-pace viper but allows it to die before she can return it to its mother, she unwittingly sets off a centuries long war between humans and snakes, with both sides suffering devastating casualties. Again, stepping back by both sides is key to solving the conflict: the snakes agree to allow their beautiful patterns to be used by the Bunun for formal clothing while the Bunun people also treat the snakes with dignity and respect, the Bunun go so far as to call them "friends".

The story, the Hunter's Faith basically follows the above-mentioned logic. Greed, arrogance, and disobedience of the forces of nature will eventually lead to destruction.

Conflicts among people, or among ethnic groups are generally more difficult to resolve than conflicts between the heavens and humans or between nature and humans as illustrated in The Story of Adal. Adal demonstrates loyalty, perseverance, wit and courage, all traditional characteristics of Bunun women. Not only did she successfully bring her son Diang back to his home, through Adal's nurturing, Diang had acquired the traits of a respected tribal leader. Finally, Adal left after having transformed into a nightingale. Adal is a model of loyalty for traditional Bunun women.

01

與月亮的約定

> 兩輪熾熱的太陽讓萬物萎靡,一對父子為了全人類的生存,歷經千辛萬苦,合力將一個太陽射瞎成為月亮,並且與月亮有了神聖的約定。從此,布農族人推行一連串的生命禮俗、祭儀與禁忌,謹記和月亮的約定,不敢違背。

在太古時候，有兩個太陽在天空輪流照射著整個大地，熾熱發燙的高溫，使得植物和動物都很不容易生長、繁殖。

有一戶布農族人家，為了取得一家活命所需的糧食，冒著酷熱在旱地裡埋頭耕作，下田時只能把小嬰兒放在田邊，再用摘來的野菇婆芋葉子為他遮住強光，避免日曬。

但是，在強烈的日光照射下，葉子很快就被曬得焦黑。

小嬰兒的父親改用香蕉葉來遮蔽太陽光，但過一會兒也燒焦了；讓人感到意外和氣憤的是，小嬰兒竟然也被曬死，變成一隻蜥蜴。

小嬰兒的父親既悲傷又生氣，他決定為全人類的生存，向太陽宣戰，把太陽射下來。

於是，父親和大兒子帶著小米等等簡單的糧食，出發射太陽去了。

 What's more?

太古：布農族人心目中的太古是一個神蹟的時代，任何事情都可能發生且令人意想不到。

太陽（vali，發利）：相較於月亮，太陽在布農族人的心中並無特殊的象徵。

變成蜥蜴：表示陽光相當熾熱，嬰兒因而被曬乾成蜥蜴，變成蜥蜴，蜥蜴布農語為「蜥蜥問」（sisiun）。

甜橘樹（izuk，以入）：父子出發前栽種甜橘樹，到射下太陽回鄉時，甜橘樹已成熟結果，表示父子射日花了很長的時間。甜橘是一種柚類植物，故事採集者杜石鑾曾於1996年前往南投縣信義鄉郡大溪左岸隆客板舊部落時，在達給呼釀氏（taki hunang）的廢棄墟厝旁邊發現一棵甜橘樹，目前在台灣北部桃、竹、苗一帶還有農夫栽種，客家人通常用這種果類祭拜神祇。

他們在出發不久後的途中，種下了一棵甜橘樹，隨即快速往太陽升起的地方前進，日復一日，到處尋找適當的地點，以便伺機射擊太陽。

不知道走了多久，父子倆走到一個視野遼闊的高處，隨時在等待日出的瞬間。驀然，他們清楚地看到太陽正漸漸升起，就準備瞄準，拉弓射擊。

但是，太陽光愈來愈強，十分刺眼，始終無法張開眼睛瞄準。最後，他們摘起山棕葉，遮蔽太陽光的照射，並從葉縫中拉起弓箭射出，成功的一舉射中太陽的左眼。

父子拉弓射中了太陽，眼看被射中的太陽，由於一隻眼睛受傷，光度慢慢減弱，盈缺變化逐漸變成月亮。

太陽被父子倆射瞎了左眼！

這時候，整個大地開始起了變化，分出了白天與夜晚，這個被射瞎的太陽就是後來我們所看到的「月亮」，她出現時就是夜晚；另一個太陽出現時就是白天。

 What's more?

山棕葉（asik，阿夕）：山棕樹是低海拔的耐陰植物，果實外觀透紅，澀中帶甜，其嫩莖味美是可口的野菜。早期台灣常取來做成掃帚、簑衣；布農族人出外工作時常將編好的山棕葉披在背上防止日曬。

月亮（buan，布岸）：布農族是一個泛靈的信仰社會，每個東西身上都有一個靈，月亮也是。月亮與布農族人密切相關，他們將月亮當作神靈，並以月亮的變化來計算時間，相近於今天的農曆，從上弦月、月圓到下弦月都有獨特的意義，就連月亮周圍的星星和月暈也有不同的意義。

由於白天只有一個太陽，氣候變得較為陰涼；夜晚和白天更是有了明顯的不同，很快的，整個山、川、動、植物的生態全都因此而改變了。

射中太陽的父子已經完成任務，正高興地準備回部落時，卻被太陽給逮住。

父子倆不斷的奔逃，好不容易從太陽的指縫中逃了出來，但終究還是被發現。

太陽將口水沾在指頭上，把他們黏住，再提到掌心上，父子倆害怕得全身發抖，但太陽卻異常平靜地對他們說：

「為什麼把我射傷成這個樣子呢？我不想報復或殺死你們，但是我要和你們約定三個戒律，回去以後告訴族人務必遵守，否則全族將會滅亡。」

「第一、要觀察我的出沒和盈缺變化，並且透過各種祭儀來紀念我，我將護祐小米及農作物豐收不虞匱乏。」

「第二、制定禁忌，規範各種不當行為，建立一個有秩序的公義社會。」

「第三、所有的人從生到死，都要舉行生命祭儀，敬告天地精靈，使人類存在有價值。」

 What's more?

祭儀（lusan，魯斯岸）：布農族人以月亮的變化計算祭儀的時間。

禁忌（samu，沙目）：布農族人最早的禁忌源自於跟月亮訂立，不能違反，後來拓展到各層面，如生活、食物、語言、親族之間婚姻的禁忌等等，但部落間的禁忌會稍有差異。

生命祭儀：布農族人從一出生到死亡都與祭典有關，利用各種禮俗賦予意義，出生祭、嬰兒祭（童子慶典）、射耳祭（打耳祭）、驅疫祭、婚俗、喪葬等等，詳見部落百寶盒中的介紹。

父子倆表示願意遵守才被釋放。

父子倆帶著月亮的戒律，經過若干年的長途跋涉，終於回到部落，看到了出發當時所種的甜橘，如今已長成大樹，樹上還結滿香甜、豐碩的果實。

他們從來沒有忘記和月亮的約定，第一件事召集所有的布農族人，說：

「從今後我們必須嚴守被射下左眼的太陽的戒律。」

「她每三十天左右出現一次，每次出現必須行使祭儀！」

「人類的生命過程，也要有禮俗，並且必須設立各種禁忌，規範一切言行。只要這樣做，我們布農族人將永遠昌隆。」

「若不遵守，全族將會滅亡。」

從此以後，布農族便展開一連串的生命禮俗、歲時祭儀，以及種種複雜的禁忌，形成了今天布農族的規律、祭祀、禁忌的由來。

Where did it come from?
本故事由採集者至南投縣信義鄉豐丘部落（salitung）採集而來。

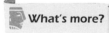

What's more?

布農族人的故地：一般指的是（lamungan，拉莫岸），約在今日南投縣竹山、名間之間一帶。但在本故事裡父子當時居住的部落與「拉莫岸」並無任何關係。

生命禮俗、歲時儀祭：布農族並沒有將生命禮俗與歲時儀祭分開，二者統稱為（lusan，魯斯岸），人類學家為了解布農族文化而將兩者加以區分。生命禮俗包括懷孕、生育、命名、嬰兒、射耳、成年、結婚、死亡等等；歲時儀祭包括開墾、播種、除草、祓除、驅鳥、收穫、貯藏等等

02

布農之女阿朵兒

被阿美族人擄走的阿朵兒未曾忘記部落的一
切，更以機智與過人的勇氣帶領兒子迪樣回
到故鄉，重回布農族人懷抱。最後，阿朵兒
雖然幻化成夜鶯離迪樣而去，但迪樣卻從阿
朵兒身上學習到了足以成為領袖的機智與勇
氣，也學習尊重他人，建立安寧且與世無爭
的布農部落。

從前，「出草」獵人頭曾經是布農族與異族爭奪獵場空間的戰爭行為，也是布農族男子獲取社會地位的重要方式之一。

位在台灣中部山區的布農族部落，時常受到來自日出地方的阪達浪獵頭隊的攻擊。

阪達浪獵頭隊在襲擊布農族時，發現一位名叫阿朵兒的美麗布農族女孩。阿朵兒年輕貌美的體態，就像春末的小米穗一樣，令人感到心曠神怡，阪達浪獵頭隊便強行擄走了阿朵兒。

可憐的阿朵兒！她才和部落一位善於彈弓琴的青年結婚，而且還懷孕了，卻活生生和丈夫分開。

被阪達浪獵頭隊俘虜的阿朵兒，沿路大聲哭喊，並因極力嘗試掙脫而全身疲憊不堪，不過仍然保持冷靜，靠著堅強的意志力，不停地使勁折彎或折斷沿途樹枝，做為日後回部落的記號。

折騰了四天之後，阿朵兒被帶到阪達浪的沙巴頂部落。

 What's more?

日出地方：東方的意思，布農族原本居住在中央山脈以西，以整個台灣來講是屬於西邊。

阪達浪（Bandalang）：是布農族口中的阿美族。

出草（makavas，馬卡發斯）：獵人頭是戰爭行為的一種，也是布農族男子獲取社會地位的表現，自古以來即存在，直到日治時代中期才逐漸消失。

阿朵兒（Adal）：這個名字多出現在布農族（TanaPima，達納比馬）姓氏裡，屬於巒社群（Takbanuaz，達卡巴奴阿）與丹社群（Takivatan，達給娃旦）系統，大約是在中央山脈郡大溪一帶。

弓琴（qangqang，剛剛）：其狀如弓，彈奏時弓背含在口中，以右手彈指，音質幽怨動人。

美麗的阿朵兒來到阪達浪沙巴頂的部落後，被迫許配給沙巴頂部落的大頭目當妻子，不久後便生下一個兒子。

沙巴頂部落的大頭目，將小男孩命名為馬耀‧骨木爾，阿朵兒被部落的人改稱為伊娃旦。

不過，阿朵兒私底下都暱稱自己的兒子為迪樣。迪樣是個漂亮的小男孩，沙巴頂部落大多數的人都知道他的父親是布農族人，但是大家都隱瞞著迪樣，沒人告訴他。

迪樣漸漸長大，與沙巴頂部落的青年一樣，都必須參加各種祭典、瞭望台站崗、秀姑巒溪溪流魚撈等事務，共同分擔部落公眾事務的責任與義務。

但是，迪樣總是被部落的人奚落、排擠與冷嘲熱諷，有時候還會集體捉弄他，或是拒絕提供食物，更常在狩獵中以「誤傷」、「不是故意」為藉口來弄傷他。

隱忍多年的迪樣，有一天趁著大頭目外出時，終於忍不住流著淚向阿朵兒哭訴：「上天祖靈為什麼那麼地不公平，我完全遵守部落的規範，從來沒有偷、搶的行為，為甚麼每次參加部落活動時，總是被部落的人集體欺侮、排擠？為什麼我的命運那麼不好？我臉上是不是有缺陷？還是我做錯什麼事？」

What's more?

沙巴頂（Sabat）：在今花蓮縣瑞穗鄉舞鶴台地上，據說舞鶴村省道路旁的石柱，就是當年沙巴頂部落大頭目家的柱樑。

迪樣（Diang）：布農族人的命名以「親族連名制」為原則，迪樣的名字應繼承祖父的名字，也就是阿朵兒的布農族丈夫的父親。

魚撈：阿美族人擅長捕魚，一般用八卦網灑網捕魚，部分用定置魚簍及射魚。

阿朵兒除了安慰迪樣要繼續認真做好長輩交代的事務外，什麼也不肯多說。

不過，從那時起，阿朵兒告訴迪樣，日後只要被派去做舂小米的工作，每次記得一定要私藏一撮小米在部落西方的山腳下，還叮嚀要藏在乾燥的地方。

雖然迪樣不知道為什麼要這麼做，但還是聽從阿朵兒的吩咐，每次被派去舂小米時就會預留一撮，悄悄地藏放到西方山腳下。

經過將近一年的時間，存放在山腳下的小米已經有一大包了。有一天，部落舉行豐年祭，祭場湧進許多人，大頭目正在祭典中擔任主司祭典。

這時候，阿朵兒認為機不可失，於是叫迪樣在太陽下山時，到貯藏小米的地方等她。

迪樣雖然覺得很疑惑，但還是依約獨自前往藏小米的地方。沒多久，阿朵兒也來了，這個時候才原原本本的告訴迪樣，為什麼會一直被部落的人欺負的原因：

「迪樣，我們不是這個部落的人，我們原本就是布農族的人，當我懷你的時候，沙巴頂部落的邦達浪獵頭隊襲擊我們的故鄉，把我強行帶到這裡。

What's more?

舂小米（mabazu，馬巴入）：將小米放在臼內，再利用杵舂擊去殼。

豐年祭（hahai，哈海意）：以布農語稱阿美族的豐年祭。

主司祭典（paliskadan lusan，巴利斯嘎難 魯斯岸）：是部落中專司祭儀者，但不包括作戰的祭儀，類似阿美族掌管整個部落所有事情，包括祭典、作戰的頭目。

所以，你是布農族人！今天，我要帶你回到我們的故鄉，不要再受到阪達浪的奚落和虐待。」

迪樣這時候才恍然大悟，原來自己是布農族人，所以才會受到種種不公平且無情的待遇。

迪樣下定決心和阿朵兒一起回到布農族人的懷抱。

於是，阿朵兒仔細辨認當初自己所折彎的樹枝，以及樹枝折斷後所長出的新枝葉，帶著迪樣循著這些記號，翻越重重山徑，朝著西方，往自己的部落前進。

在逃出沙巴頂部落的第二天下午，遠處不斷傳來阪達浪部落追兵及狗吠聲，而且狗吠聲愈來愈近，似乎就快追上了。

聰明的阿朵兒，在驚險中立刻帶著迪樣快速跑到附近的大瀑布，躲進水濂內洞穴。由於瀑布水流阻絕了氣味，狗兒無法嗅出他們的行蹤，阿朵兒與迪樣因此逃過一劫。

擺脫追兵後，阿朵兒和迪樣拖著疲憊的步伐，不分日夜走了幾天，朝著回家的路前進。

這一天，夜深寂靜，阿朵兒藉著明亮的月光，找到昔日熟悉、懷念許久的家園。

正當阿朵兒牽著迪樣的手尋找昔日的家園時，他們聽到不遠處飄來熟悉的弓琴聲。原來是阿朵兒的丈夫，正在拉彈弓琴，唱著思念阿朵兒的幽怨詩曲。

阿朵兒含著眼淚，握緊迪樣的手，向琴聲飄來之處狂奔而去，在看到她的丈夫時，卻發現他已續絃，身旁已有別人。

就在此時，迪樣驚覺自己手裡的溫度消失了，轉瞬間阿朵兒從迪樣的視線中消失不見，直到迪樣聽到遠處夜鶯的悲鳴：「沙布斯　盎、沙布斯盎……」

迪樣從恍惚中驚覺，原來母親阿朵兒已經幻化成夜鶯了。不禁悲從中來，跪地哭號，「迪那！迪那！」但是，阿朵兒再也不會回來了。

時間一天天的過去，回到布農族的迪樣漸漸長大成人，由於他的閱歷豐富，又嚴守部落規範，再加上勤勞、孝順，深受布農族人的愛戴，很快被推舉為氏族中的軍事領袖「拉飛安」。

炎夏的某天，迪樣舉行占卜之後，卜出大吉的好兆頭，於是迪樣決定組織一支布農族獵頭隊，朝著東方阪達浪沙巴頂部落前進。

 What's more?

幽怨詩曲：布農族平時有所謂「敘述寂寞之歌」（pisdadaidaz，比斯搭泰大爾），利用哀愁的歌聲敘述失去兒子、思念親人、自己命運坎坷之苦。

丈夫已續絃：阿朵兒丈夫雖愛阿朵兒，但族人判定阿朵兒已被阿美族人殺死後，便強行將另外一個女人許配給他（當時布農族結婚制是搶婚），但阿朵兒的丈夫並不喜歡她，仍朝思暮想著阿朵兒，常常拉彈著弓琴思念故人。

沙布斯－盎（salbu isang）：其中salbu是哀愁的意思，isang是心的意思，表示非常悽涼難過。salbu isang也就是布農語中的夜鶯，因為叫聲而命名。

迪那（tina）：母親的意思。

當他們潛入沙巴頂部落，正好也是部落豐年祭的最後一天，警戒非常鬆懈，很輕易找到大頭目正在家中附近的大石頭上納涼著。夏夜的圓月高掛，迪樣毫不猶豫立刻襲擊大頭目，並完成獵頭，連夜返回布農部落。

族人知道這個好消息，都很高興迪樣不僅為阿朵兒報仇，也為布農族人洗雪前恥。

由於迪樣特殊的成長經驗，讓他學會誠實地接納境遇波折的人，知道如何尊重他人，並很珍惜的積極參與部落各種祭典及氏族活動，和家庭、氏族、部落之間建立了良好的互動關係。

中年以後的迪樣，被推舉為全部落的「拉飛安」；在他的帶領之下，成為非常安寧而無紛爭的部落，深受世世代代頌揚。

Where did it come from?

本故事由採集者至花蓮縣萬榮鄉馬遠部落採集而來。

What's more?

軍事領袖：（lavian，拉飛安）

占卜（pistasiy，比斯他斯意）：布農族的占卜會因目的不同而由不同的人進行占卜。祭典占卜是祭司，獵首則由軍事領袖進行。占卜方式先做鳥占，配合當天晚上的夢占以及行進間各種景物表現出來的現象。

 憤怒的百步蛇

布農族婦女卡布斯向母百步蛇乞求帶回一隻小百步蛇，作為編織服飾的參考圖案，但是小百步蛇卻死了。於是，布農族遭到百步蛇群攻擊，族人死傷無數，也引來雙方世代挾怨報復。

還好後來布農族人和百步蛇以智慧化解危機，約定從此是朋友，大家和平共處。

從前在布農族的部落裡，有一對非常相愛的夫妻，妻子叫卡布斯，丈夫名叫比馬。

卡布斯平時主內，負責管教子女、料理食物、採集附近的野菜、編織衣服，並打理家中大大小小雜事。比馬就負責對外事務與重大工作，包括打獵、出草、耕作，以及參加部落的祭典活動。

卡布斯非常深愛她的丈夫比馬，因此，希望能幫他裁織合身而美麗的衣服，若穿著參加部落祭典和各種公眾事務，一定會受到族人們的稱讚與尊重，自己也將加倍感到光榮。

怎麼樣的衣服花色最美麗呢？卡布斯想了很久，把各種動物做了一番比較後，覺得百步蛇的圖案與色澤最高貴豔麗，便打算利用這種特殊圖案來編織比馬的服飾。

有一天，卡布斯遇到一隻母的百步蛇。

卡布斯立刻大膽的前去和母蛇商量，希望能借一隻小百步蛇作為編織服飾的圖案。

起初，母百步蛇不同意，但禁不起卡布斯一再乞求，終於勉強同意。

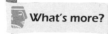

What's more?

公眾事務：如部落祭典、做部落飲用水的工作。

百步蛇（kaviaz，卡飛阿）：是朋友的意思，當稱為「卡飛」（gavit）則是誓約的意思。布農族人將百步蛇視為朋友，不能殺，看到牠要撕一塊衣服給牠，並跟牠說：「你快點走！」布農族撕衣服的舉動，是友誼，也是禮物。

母百步蛇答應讓卡布斯帶一隻小百步蛇回家，作為卡布斯編織服飾的參考圖案，但是約定好在第七天時要把小百步蛇還給牠。

過了幾天，卡布斯終於織好衣服，鄰居的婦女看到卡布斯編了這麼漂亮的衣服，也想學她用百步蛇圖案來編織，便向卡布斯借小百步蛇參考；於是，鄰居的婦女也編了一件件美麗的男服。

消息傳遍整個部落，有更多的婦女都想來借那隻小百步蛇，就在你爭我搶的過程中，竟然不小心把小百步蛇折騰死了。

日子一天一天過去，與母百步蛇約定的第七天到了。母百步蛇來到卡布斯家中，向卡布斯要回小百步蛇，但是卡布斯無法依約交出，便隨口說：

「現在沒辦法馬上給你，可以等到明天再還吧！」

到了第二天，母百步蛇再來取回小百步蛇，卡布斯以借給別人為理由，又再度表示無法交還。

母百步蛇聽了後非常不滿並撂下狠話：

「你們這些殺我孩子又不守信用的布農族人，給我當心！」說完就離去。

What's more?

男服：布農族男、女的衣服有所差異，男子沒有褲子的設計，以丁帶來替代，這是為了在狩獵或征戰時，行動能夠靈巧、敏捷的應付突發的狀況，上衣為背心，胸前有一胸袋可置放小物品，如菸葉、菸斗、肉脯。女子上身為短衣長袖，衣邊繡有花紋，下身圍繞一圈半的圍裙，長及小腿處，女性的服飾有頭飾及綁腿。

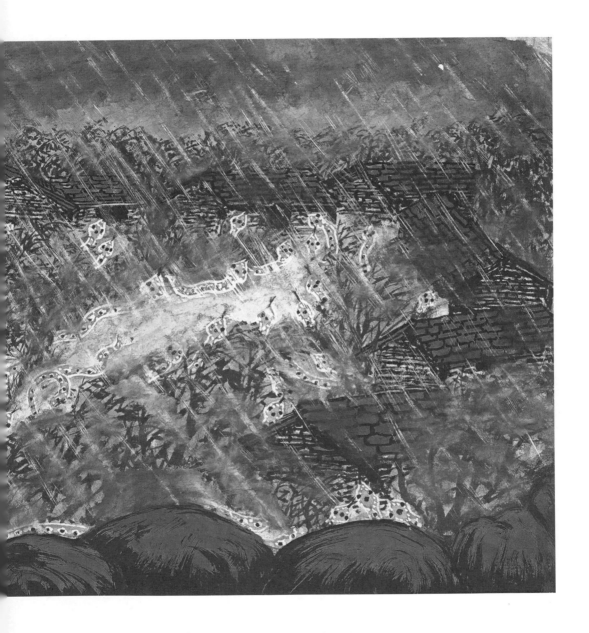

有一天夜晚，部落刮起了大颱風，大雨滂沱；但是布農族人都睡的很熟，毫未注意有任何異狀。

這時候，一群一群的百步蛇在狂風暴雨中，悄悄地湧入部落裡。

成群的百步蛇肆無忌憚地進入每一族人家中，遇到人就咬，憤怒的把儲藏了一整個冬天的毒液注入人體內，大部分熟睡的族人毒發而死。

成群的百步蛇開始出沒於田野、小徑、獵場等處，只要遇到人就立刻主動攻擊，許多族人在出外時都被無情突襲身亡；這個大災難讓部落幾乎損失一半以上的人口。

布農族人不甘如此被屠殺滅族，開始全體動員起來，誓言無論何時何地，只要遇到百步蛇，一定要用把牠們活活打死，並且隨地棄置，表示報復。

幾個世代下來，布農族人與百步蛇都死傷慘重。雙方逐漸互相開始反省，如果繼續長期互相仇視，必然莫可奈何的同歸於盡，於是嘗試提出妥協之道。

經過一番商討後，雙方決定，百步蛇同意把自身美麗的圖案交給布農族，做為正式服裝的圖樣，並且不再隨意攻擊布農族人；布農族人更是承諾，不但不可再屠殺，且將改為以嚴肅、尊重的態度善待百步蛇。

Where did it come from?
本故事由採集者至南投縣信義鄉潭南部落採集而來。

雙方因為有了這樣的約定，從此開始和平共存。

後來，布農族人對百步蛇便有兩種解釋：稱做「卡飛」表示誓約；若稱做「卡飛阿」，指的是朋友的意思。

直到現在，從布農族的傳統服飾的底色、條紋及製作方式，仍然可以明顯地看出，都是以百步蛇的顏色及花紋為主要圖案，延用到今天！

04

獵人的信仰

不認輸的獵人們與大自然抗爭而慘遭不幸。
人類應該尊重自然，切勿心存破壞與貪婪，
或者不顧危險而導致死難。要保有尊重自然
與大地的權力，唯有與大自然和諧共處才是
人類之福。

布農族從前有一個稱為麥阿桑部落，每到收穫月與開墾月之間，也就是打獵的月份，部落的成年男士會開始前往自己的獵場，打獵或採集有用植物。

有一天，某氏族獵隊依慣例在舉行獵祭後，由獵人們帶著幾隻土狗一起圍捕獵物。這次，有位獵人帶了一個未成年的小孩參加。

到達獵寮後，獵人們每天都在團捕野鹿，並將辛苦捕獲的獵物帶回獵寮裡頭存放。

幾天之後，天氣然有了變化，看來似乎是強烈颱風逼近，眾人議論紛紛，最後決定立刻停止狩獵，盡快趕回部落。

這時，帶小孩的獵人主張，為了大家的安全，不宜冒險，應該避過風雨之後再做打算。

多數人認為，這樣是懦夫的行為，幾乎異口同聲地說：

「這雨風算什麼！再危險的情況我們都經歷過，這有什麼了不起！」

於是收拾東西便匆匆踏上歸程，一些對於留下非常不以為然的獵人，不但在臨走前將食物、獵物全部帶走，更將獵寮的火熄滅，打算讓他們父子自生自滅。

What's more?

打獵的月分：大月在九、十月間，打獵的月份也是訓練出草的好日子，布農族的武力訓練、打獵、射箭也是利用這段時間來進行。

眾人一離開,帶著小孩的父親,立刻跑到火塘旁,努力在剛被熄滅的炭火中翻找,很幸運地在死角處發現,還有幾個尚未完全熄滅的木頭火星。因此,立刻把乾柴堆放在一起,拚命吹出火花燃燒起來,就這樣取暖安然度過這個颱風夜。

第二天,當風雨稍減,兒子在獵寮附近看到一隻可能被是落石壓死的水鹿,父子倆趁著餘火烤熟,填飽了肚子。不久,太陽光漸漸浮現,澗溪的水也慢慢退了,牠們就揹起吃剩的肉脯,循著獵路返回部落。

回途中,父子倆很意外的發現,前幾天大膽冒險回部落的族人,竟然已經全部死亡,有些人更是血肉模糊,屍體東一塊、西一塊,可見當時風雨一定非常強烈。

這位父親為了紀念這些獵友,就將發現各個屍塊的地方,個別以身體部位來命名,以警惕後人,要嚴肅敬重大自然無窮的神秘力量,不要以為「人定勝天」而隨意破壞,以免帶來死難。

Where did it come from?
本故事由採集者至南投縣信義鄉豐丘部落(salitung)採集而來。

What's more?

火塘(巴檸,banin):煮飯的地方。

肉脯(凱里旺,qailivan):乾肉。

部落百寶盒 ┃┃ 傳授哈「原」秘笈，搖身變成布農通

一、木刻畫曆

「木刻畫曆」是布農文化之寶，也是台灣原住民族群中唯一有「文字」表徵的歷史文物。根據文獻記載，1937年（日本統治時期），此一長約122.7公分、寬約11.8公分、厚2.4公分的木刻，在今日位於南投縣境內的布農族卡尼多岸社（Qanituan）頭目塔魯姆‧滿來旺（Talum Mangdavan）家被發現，畫曆上記載著各項重要農事及祭典活動的日期與事項。

木刻畫曆在日本時代被稱為「繪曆」，布農族的祭司用這個繪曆來記錄祭典時間。祭司在記錄前會先與其他部落的祭司商討約定，採用同樣的符號來記錄，在交接給下一個祭司前，也會仔細交代如何記錄。

開墾祭　　　　播栗祭　　　栗 收穫祭　除草祭　　打耳祭

▶ 布農族人的生活濃縮紀錄

台灣原住民多無自己的文字，所以他們用口耳相傳的方式，很小心的傳下族群的歷史，或是祖先的教訓、生活的經驗；他們也把祖先重要的事蹟編成歌謠，藉著祭典等場合，一代一代的傳唱下去。

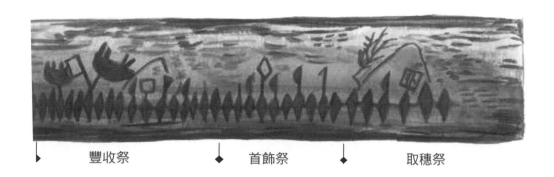

▶　豐收祭　　　◆　首飾祭　　　◆　取穗祭

布農族以觀察月亮的盈缺來耕作、舉行祭典，發明出自己的「行事曆」。這塊木刻畫曆也稱為「記事曆板」，以記號、圖形、象形、符號記錄部落的祭典時間和生產活動，等於是布農族人全年生活內容的濃縮，意象簡明易懂，已經是原始文字的雛形。這塊木刻畫曆標明了重要祭典與活動，有墾地、整地祭典日、播種粟米的祭儀、粟米收穫祭、除草祭儀、打耳祭、豐收祭等等。

下列是「木刻畫曆」中一部分的記號與其所代表的意義：

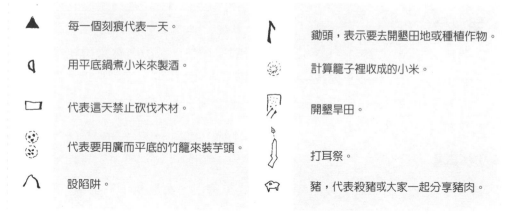

▲　每一個刻痕代表一天。　　　　　　　鋤頭，表示要去開墾田地或種植作物。

ʠ　用平底鍋煮小米來製酒。　　　　　　計算籠子裡收成的小米。

▭　代表這天禁止砍伐木材。　　　　　　開墾旱田。

　　代表要用廣而平底的竹籠來裝芋頭。　打耳祭。

⋀　設陷阱。　　　　　　　　　　　　　豬，代表殺豬或大家一起分享豬肉。

二、祭典豐富的布農族

布農族是台灣原住民當中，活動地區廣、移動相當頻繁的族群。因為身處高山，對於自然界的威力與變化十分敬畏，也產生了許多的忌諱、巫術、神話、祭典等傳統文化與宗教行為。

由於布農族沒有最高信仰的神，從出生到死亡都與祭典有關，希望利用各種禮俗提醒族人重視生命的意義與存在的價值；所以說，泛靈信仰與繁複的農業祭儀和生命禮儀，是布農族文化的一大特色。布農族人從出生到死亡都與祭典有關，利用各種禮俗賦予意義。

▶ 出生祭

嬰兒在出生的那一刻，會舉行一個簡短的「出生祭」儀式，僅僅是短暫的祈福、禱告，並沒有特定的儀式，重點在於對天感恩的祝禱。與每年7、8、9月間舉行的嬰兒祭不同。

在嬰兒出生後約一個月（若嬰兒於月圓出生，時間為下個月月圓時；若於月缺時出生，則時間為下個月月缺），以非常隆重的儀式，請部落中擅長狩獵、行為受族人尊敬的長老為小孩「命名」，取名者需於前一天舉行夢占，若得吉夢，才可進行「命名」，到時家人必須全部盛裝參與。

▶ 嬰兒祭

布農族人認為，每年7、8、9月間舉行的嬰兒祭，象徵著尊重傳統文化與生命的重大意義，是最重要也最具有代表性的生命禮俗。祭典當天，過去一年內所有新生嬰兒都會有掛項鍊的儀式，祈禱嬰兒平安長大；這是屬於家族性的祭典，不需要有祭司。

▶ 成年禮

到孩童成年（約16歲）後，會舉行「成年禮」，布農語「柄都散」（bintu-san），邀請有拔牙經驗的長老，替少年們拔除犬齒；以花蓮馬遠部落為例，

此傳統約在日本時代末期才漸漸式微。經過成年禮以後，女孩開始向母親學習織布，男孩必須跟從父兄上山狩獵，努力成為出色的獵人。

▶ 打耳祭

打耳祭是布農族一年中最盛大的祭典活動，舉行的時間大約在4、5月間、小米除草祭以後的閒暇時間，確切日期則由祭司決定。打耳祭又稱射耳祭，布農語「馬拉卡泰那」（malaqtainga），有著薪火相傳、教育、競技、團結、法律等等意義與功能。

打耳祭當天的祭典相當重要，但之前的準備工作也十分隆重，過程如下：

（1）祭典前的打獵「卡奴布」（qanup）：
為了迎接重大祭典，部落男子需上山狩獵，婦女也開始配合打獵回來的時間釀製小米酒，並祈求每天晚上做豐收的吉祥之夢。因為鹿、羌和山豬是布農英雄獵取的最高榮譽目標，因此射箭活動裡，通常就以鹿及山豬的耳朵作為標靶。

（2）對空鳴槍傳訊息「帕丁哈爾」（patinqal）：
獵人在祭典前一天下午返家，下山前會先從山頂上對空鳴槍，然後一路大聲齊唱或輪唱，通知全部落的人。

（3）迎接獵人「馬丁帕斯度」（matinpasdu）：
家人在與獵人們事先約定的地方等候，獻上小米酒慰勞辛勞，獵人也拿出剛捕獲烤熟的新鮮肉乾與家人分享，大家高聲唱歌返家。

（4）祭獵槍「比斯拉賀」（pislahi）：
打耳祭當天，凌晨雞啼時，獵人們就帶著自己的獵具，到祭司家中集合，舉行祭槍儀式。大家把狩獵器具放在地上，分兩列圍蹲在祭司兩側，由祭司領唱祭槍歌，祈求獵物都會被這些槍捕獲，以及獵人打獵都

能平安順利大豐收。

（5）獵骨祭「馬巴非士」（mapatvis）：

祭槍完畢後，就在放置野獸下巴骨的地方，舉行獵骨祭，只有祭司及今年獵取最多獵物的人才能進入。祭司帶領參與者以儀式安慰獵物的靈魂，並祈求牠們為部落引來更多的獵物，接著由這位最英勇的獵人將下巴骨掛起來，呈獻成果。

（6）射耳「馬巴那泰那」（mapanaktainga）：

祭祀完畢後，部落的人們到射耳場上集合，由長老們開始拉弓放箭，射向預先準備的野獸耳朵。長老射完後再換男孩們射，長老們也會協助拉不動弓箭的男孩拉開弓箭。男孩們都射完之後，就由成年男子上場。

（7）祈求孩童成為英雄「都虎米斯」（tauqumis）：

長老會將肉分給男孩們，並且揉吹男孩的耳朵，同時祈禱他們成為英雄。

（8）分吃祭拜過的烤肉「馬巴希奴爾」（mapasitnul）：

射耳活動結束後，族人會分吃祭拜過的烤肉，這時要確實清點人數，分肉時不可剩餘或不足，否則會被認為是不祥之兆。

（9）報戰功「馬拉斯達邦」（malastapan）：

分吃祭拜過的烤肉後，接著開始喝酒、唱歌，舉行誇功宴，誇耀自己的英勇，直到天黑才解散，布農族人全年中最盛大的祭典就此結束。

打耳祭是布農族男女都可以參加的族群活動，但男子仍然是祭典活動的主體，例如替男童揉吹耳朵，是為了驅邪祈福；射耳是希望男童早日成為布農神箭手，祭槍為求狩獵豐收，誇功宴有鼓舞士氣的涵義。

除了生命禮俗，布農族一年四季的農事祭儀也相當豐富，以下列出一年的歲時祭典：

祭典名稱	舉行時間（陽曆）	祭典意義
除草祭	1 月	除草，祈求穀物茂盛成長。
驅疫祭	4 月	驅逐惡鬼、疾病，祈求族人平安。
打耳祭	4 月～5 月	布農族最隆重、盛大的祭典，祈求狩獵豐收。
收穫祭	6 月～7 月	收割農作物的祭典儀式。
開墾祭	10 月～11 月	尋找新耕地、開始農耕。
小米播種祭	11 月～12 月	告知祖靈即將播種，並祝禱小米豐收。
甘薯祭	11 月～12 月	告知祖靈種植地瓜等作物。
進倉祭	11 月	將小米存入米倉，祈禱祖靈保護不腐壞。

詳細祭典時間可聯絡布農族所分布的各縣市政府：

· 台東縣政府 電話：089-326141，網址http://www.taitung.gov.tw/

· 花蓮縣政府 電話：03-8227171，網址http://www.hlhg.gov.tw/

· 高雄縣政府 電話：07-7477611，網址http://www.kscg.gov.tw/

· 南投縣政府 電話：049-2222106，網址http://www.nthg.gov.tw/

＊ 布農族主要分佈圖，請見封面裏頁。

三、天籟八部合音享譽國際

1943年，日本音樂學者黑澤隆朝教授曾來台對原住民音樂做實地的調查與錄音，在當時的台東鳳山郡里壠山社（現今台東縣海端鄉崁頂村）首次發現了布農族的「巴希布布」（pasibutbut）小米豐收祈禱歌中泛音的半音階唱法，在民族音樂學上引起了極大的震撼。在音樂史上，一直都是先由一個音、兩個音、三個音逐漸演化而成，但是，布農族的合音唱法是他們自古流傳至今的歌謠，演唱方式非常特殊，是以多聲部和音唱法，從低音漸高，一直唱到最高音域的和諧音，一般人稱為「八部合音」，如此複雜豐富的合音讓人訝異！

1952年，黑澤教授將錄音發表，受到國際著名的音樂學者及世界民族音樂界的重視，並被譽為人間天籟，是人類珍貴的文化資產，這是布農族音樂蜚聲國際的一個開始。

布農族獨特的合唱技巧，起因於居住環境較其他族群疏落，並且聚落大多沿溪流建立，有事常以歌聲呼朋引伴，不覺中締造了如此美妙動人的合音。他們也將祭儀音樂視為神聖之聲，藉由虔敬的歌聲獻給天神，感動上天。

八部合音並非有八部合唱，只是用較複雜的合唱方式來進行，用於布農族1月份播種祭到3月份除草祭期間所演唱的曲子。播種祭前，由祭司決定祭日，接著慎選族中這一年之內未違背禁忌的數名成年男子，在祭典前一天住在祭屋內，並享用最佳的美食。次日，祭司帶領這些成年男子在家屋外，面向圓心圍成圓圈，雙手伸開，穿插在身旁族人的背後腰際間，緩緩逆時鐘方向移動。圓圈內會放置種米一串，在祭司的領唱下，演唱從屋外再慢慢移入屋內，祈禱今年播種的小米能豐收堆滿穀倉。

▶ 演唱方式

演唱方式先由低音領唱者以「嗚」發出長音，其他歌者再分成二部或三部以三度、四度、五度的距離反覆進行；高聲部依領唱者所發的音延續，慢慢循音階上升，一直唱到他們認為最完美的和諧圓滿、祖靈已可接受的境界才一起停下來，這也就是天神最滿意的合音。

布農族人相信，歌唱的好壞與否與當年小米收成的豐歉有關，在演唱中途如果不合音或不順暢便為不吉祥之兆，因此演唱此曲時，族人必須嚴守禁忌、態度嚴肅、全力以赴。

▶ 布農族樂器

布農族除了合音優美外，還會運用一些樂器，大致有弓琴、口簧琴、弦琴、木杵等。

弓琴是布農族人最主要的樂器，將長條竹片彎曲成弓，再以一根鐵弦繫在竹弓兩端，演奏方式如現今的吉他，多半用來自娛。

口簧琴，也稱繩口琴，布農族人利用繩子的抽拉振動簧片，並藉著吹氣及吸氣，使琴產生共鳴發出聲音。吹奏速度緩慢、樂音悠長而清晰，最能抒發個人情緒。

布農族的弦琴有四弦琴及五弦琴，琴的下方大都有一個共鳴箱（中空的鐵箱或是容器）；有時候若沒有共鳴箱，也可以直接用手挑彈琴弦。主要用來自我娛樂或抒發心情。

布農族的杵樂，是以長短、粗細不同的木杵敲擊石板或石塊，所發出的聲音時高亢、時低沉，是相當純樸的聲音。

四、布農族的分布與社會組織

布農族的布農（bunun），指「人」的意思，布農族是生活在高山的族群，大部分生活在海拔1500公尺以上的高地，分布於台灣中央山脈兩側的南投、高雄、花蓮、台東等山地。在東南亞許多民族中，可說是分布地區海拔最高、最適於高山生活的一族；故有中央山脈的統治者或守護者，及典型的高山民族之稱。

▸ 分布地點

布農族分布廣，依語言、祭典儀式的差異，大致可以分為五大社群，目前各群居住地分別如下：

卓社群（Takitudu，達給督度）：分布在南投縣仁愛鄉、信義鄉，濁水溪上游沿岸山地，是布農族群居住地的最北邊。

社群（Takibakha，達給巴哈）：大部分居住於南投縣境內仁愛、信義兩鄉。

丹社群（Takivatan，達給娃旦）：居住於南投縣信義鄉、花蓮縣萬榮鄉、瑞穗鄉、豐濱鄉、台東縣長濱鄉。

巒社群（Takbanuaz，達卡巴奴阿）：分布在南投縣信義鄉，花蓮縣瑞穗、卓溪鄉，台東縣海端鄉、延平鄉，高雄縣桃源鄉、三民鄉。

郡社群（Isbukun，伊斯布滾）：是五個社群中最大的一支，分布於南投縣信義鄉，台東縣海端鄉、延平鄉及高雄縣三民、桃源鄉。

▸ 社會組織

布農族是典型的父系社會，以氏族部落為組織中心，原則上都由老人擔任統治的領袖，領袖之下有部落長老會議。

完整的布農部落裡，有三位領導人物：

一、主持各項農事祭儀的祭司。

二、巫師，可以占卜未來世界，具有治病、心理治療、婚姻諮詢等功能，同時也是部落裡糾紛協調者、裁定者。

三、軍事領袖，負責征戰、獵首，是勇士、也是對外作戰的指揮者。通常沒有一定的選舉儀式，採公認推舉方式，但一定要有良好的道德操守。

五、布農族的傳統服飾

相較於其他族群，布農族的服飾顯得樸實簡單，顯示出該族長期生活於海拔1000公尺以上的高地，遵循自然環境與生態的平衡；也顯露出布農族人樸實、內斂的民族性。

傳統上布農族織布是屬於女性的工作，男人更有不能碰觸織布機的禁忌，但獸皮衣飾的揉皮工作，則是由男人來擔任。布農族早期以狩獵為生，熟悉動物的習性，更能依據野獸皮的特性，製作成各種不同的服飾，保暖族人的身體。

▶ 項鍊

布農族在飾品上也有男、女的差異，值得一提的是布農族的項鍊，具有莊嚴的宗教意涵卻無華麗的形狀。布農族人的傳統項鍊大致分為「孩童項鍊」、「破除項鍊」和「獵人項鍊」三種。因為項鍊從祭典儀式衍生，所以隱藏消災解厄和天神的祝福的意義。嬰兒祭中有一重要的儀式是為新生兒「掛項鍊」，期望孩子們能像項鍊般耀眼、美麗。

▶ 服飾

布農族的服裝與飾品有男、女的區別：

男子的服飾：

1.男子沒有褲子的設計，以一片類似裙子的布來替代，這是為了在狩獵或征戰時，行動能夠靈巧、敏捷以應付突發的狀況。

2.上衣前襟為無袖之兩片長褂，長度到腹部為背心，到膝蓋則為長袍。

3.胸前有一胸袋可置放小物品，如菸葉、菸斗、肉脯；征戰、出獵則放置小匕首。方形胸袋自頸部斜掛入，並在其間織繡幾何花紋。

4.獸帽及獸皮衣是以野獸皮加工而成的服裝，這種服裝是在平日工作或上山狩獵時穿著。

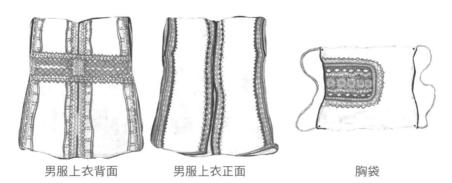

男服上衣背面   男服上衣正面   胸袋

女子的服飾：

1.上身為短衣長袖，衣邊繡有花紋邊。

2.下身著圍繞一圈半的圍裙，長及小腿處，底層接地處繡有百步蛇花紋的花邊，顏色以藍、黑色為主。

3.女性的服飾有頭飾及綁腿。

女服上衣正面   女子長裙   女子膝褲(綁腿)

造訪部落　部落藏寶圖，來挖布農寶

看過了布農族的神話與傳說故事，你是否已經了解布農族和月亮為什麼會有約定，對布農族產生什麼影響？是否感動於阿朵兒忠於部落的情懷、過人的勇氣，另外，是否也想看看布農族參考百步蛇身上花紋製成的衣服？

布農族分為五大群，主要居住在南投縣仁愛鄉、信義鄉；花蓮縣萬榮鄉、瑞穗鄉、卓溪鄉；台東縣海端鄉、延平鄉；高雄縣桃源鄉、三民鄉。在這些布農族人居住的部落裡，你都可以親自體會布農的文化，現在，透過這份精心編製的「布農族文化導覽圖」(請詳見本書第137頁)，陪伴身歷其境，邀請你盡情挖掘部落文化寶藏，保證不虛此行。

當然，造訪部落時更不能錯過布農族豐富的祭典活動，包括生命禮俗與農事祭儀，其中最為大眾所知的就是每年4至5月間舉辦的打耳祭，詳細祭典時間請洽布農族分布的縣市政府：

· 台東縣政府 電話：089-326141，網址http://www.taitung.gov.tw/

· 花蓮縣政府 電話：03-8227171，網址http://www.hlhg.gov.tw/

· 高雄縣政府 電話：07-7477611，網址http://www.kscg.gov.tw/

· 南投縣政府 電話：049-2222106，網址http://www.nthg.gov.tw/

布農族
文化導覽圖

族語開口說　　**入境隨俗的布農語**

很高興見到你！
Manaskal i　maqtu mapunaqtung suuh!
馬那斯尬 伊 馬杜　馬布那凍　　　蘇幹
高興　　　　　可以　遇見　　　　你

我也是。你好啊！
Maupa amin.　Miquhmisag!
帽爸　阿命　米古米散
同樣　全部。 祝福你(你好)！

請問貴姓大名？
Tukauwun su ngan?
讀高汶　　蘇 楨
如何稱呼 你 名字

我的名字叫做阿浪‧滿來旺。
Manak ngan a　tupaun tu　Alang Manglavan.
馬那　楨 阿 讀巴汶 杜　阿浪　滿來旺
我　　名字 稱為　　　阿浪　滿來旺

你們午餐都吃什麼？
Maaq mu　tinaungquh kakaunun?
馬阿　木　迪能固　　卡高嫩
什麼 你們 中餐　　　吃

我們的主食是栗(小米)。
Manam kakaunun a sia maduq.
馬難　卡高嫩　　阿 下 馬杜
我們　常吃　　　　類 栗(小米)

你們衣服的圖案真漂亮。
Mananu maauaz mu ihan　hulus　sintinaqis　patas.
馬那怒　馬腦阿　木 伊汗 虎路斯 星底那基斯 巴塔斯
非常　　漂亮　你們 在 衣服　縫製　　　圖案

謝謝！這是百步蛇身上的圖案。
Uninang !　Maaipi a aiia kaviaz lubu tu patas.
烏尼釀　馬愛必 阿 愛夏 卡飛阿 魯布 杜 巴塔斯
感謝　　這個　關於　百步蛇 身上　圖案

這個房子特別美麗。
Mavaivi kainuazan tu lumaq.
馬菲肺　卡伊奴阿讓 杜 魯馬
特別　　美麗　　　　家屋

這是我們布農族獨特的石板屋。
Mavaivi luaq batu　asis a　Bunun.
馬菲肺 魯馬 巴度 愛希 阿 布農
特別　家屋 石板 關於　布農

你們部落什麼時候舉行打耳祭？
Laqua mu　asang malaqyainga?
拉掛　木　阿桑　馬拉卡泰那
何時　你們　部落　打耳祭

我們的部落每年四、五月間舉行。
Manam asang a ihan pat hima buan lusan.
馬拿　阿桑　阿 伊汗 巴 伊馬 布岸 魯斯岸
我們　部落　在 四 五 月 祭典

你們的合音真美。
Masling　mu　sinkahuzas.
馬斯令　木　心卡呼日朝
真好(好聽)你們 和音(唱)

布農族的八部合音聞名國際。
Minnqanan mu Bunun a　pasibutbut ihan kauba nastuti　Bunun
明安難　木 布農 阿 巴希步布 伊汗 高巴 拿斯凸弟 布農
出名　你們 布農　八部合音 在 所有 在世間(地下)人類(布農)

我很喜歡你們的部落。
Asa sk imu　tu　asan.
阿沙 阿 伊木 度 阿桑
喜歡 我 你們 部落

謝謝你的到來。
Uninang I tantunquan su.
烏尼難 伊 但東古岸 蘇
感謝 到來作客 你

很高興認識你。
Manaskal I　mapasaqal su.
馬拿斯嘎魯 伊 馬巴沙卡爾 蘇
高興 認識 你

希望能再相見！
Maqtuan muqnah mapasadu!
馬讀岸 木那 馬巴沙杜
希望 再一次 相見面

下次再見！
Tan tungua!
但 讀古阿
下次 來作客

歡迎下次再來。
Na altalak asu.
那 阿他樂 阿蘇
期待 你

本書發音採用丹社群的發音

學習加油站　**本書漢語與布農語名詞對照表**

故事01：與月亮的約定

用漢字拼讀	布農語	漢語名詞
發利	vali	太陽
布農	Bunun	布農族
呼佈	hubuq	嬰兒
布拉達一	bulaktai	姑婆芋
蜥蜥問	sisiun	蜥蜴
達馬	tama	父親
奔奔	bunbun	香蕉
布農	bunun	人類
以入	izuk	甜橘樹
烏發貳	uvazaz	兒子
阿夕	asik	山棕葉
布樹	busul	弓箭
馬大	mata	眼睛
布岸	buan	月亮
哈尼岸	hanian	白天
馬木	maqmut	黑夜
馬敵阿	matiqav	瞎
心嘎汕	sinqasam	戒律
魯斯岸	lusan	祭儀（生命禮俗、歲時儀祭）
沙目	samu	禁忌
米古米斯	miqumis	生
馬大日	madaz	死
拉莫岸	lamungan	布農族人的故地
拉斯	las	果實

故事02：布農之女阿朵兒

用漢字拼讀	布農語	漢語名詞
阪達浪	Bandalang	布農族對阿美族的稱謂
馬卡發斯	makavas	出草
阿朵兒	Adal	阿朵兒（人名）
比娜娜娃日	binanauaz	女孩
剛剛	qang qang	弓琴
麥多多阿日	mainduduaz	青年
馬巴西辣	mapasiza	結婚
安布布	anbubut	懷孕
巴那那日	bananaz	丈夫
沙巴頂	Sabat	沙巴頂（地名）
馬魯斯比岸	malusbingaz	妻子
巴那那日 烏娃阿日	bananaz uvazaz	男孩
馬耀・骨木爾	Maiyau kumul	馬耀・骨木爾（人名）
迪樣	Diang	迪樣（人名）
卡考諾	kakaunun	食物
迪合寧	dihanin	天
卡尼杜	qanitu	祖靈
達基司	daqis	臉
達司凸 伊馬	tastu ima	一撮
馬杜	maduh	小米
馬巴入	mabazu	舂小米
哈海意	hahai	布農語中阿美族的豐年祭
巴利斯嘎難 魯斯岸	paliskadan lusan	主司祭典
阿樹	asu	狗
達斯達斯	tastas	瀑布
屏凸岸	bintuqan	星
魯馬	lumaq	家
比斯搭泰大爾	pisdadaidaz	幽怨詩曲
伊馬	ima	手
沙布斯 盎	salbu isang	夜鶯
迪那	tina	母親
希落格	siluq	氏族
拉飛安	lavian	軍事領袖

故事03：憤怒的百步蛇

用漢字拼讀	布農語	漢語名詞
巴卡土斯讓	paka tuszang	夫妻
卡布斯	Qabus	卡布斯（人名）
比馬	Pima	比馬（人名）
烏佛日	uvazaz	子女
馬丁汶	matinun	編織
卡諾卜	ganup	打獵
骨拉骨拉	kuazakuza	耕作
彌尼古米斯	miniqumis	動物
卡飛阿	kaviaz	百步蛇，朋友之意
卡飛	gavit	百步蛇，誓約的意思
巴塔斯	patas	圖案
巴卡但阿	pakatanah	鄰居
魯魯灣	luvluvan	颱風
骨打難	quhdanan	雨
買浪基基諾	mailankikinuz	世代
傣尼斯尹岸	tainisian	顏色

故事04：獵人的信仰

用漢字拼讀	布農語	漢語名詞
麥阿桑	maiasang	指曾經居住過的舊部、社
阿桑	asang	部落（村莊）
卡卡奴布	qaganup	獵人
搭魯幹	taluqan	獵寮
乾旺	qanvan	野鹿
魯魯佛	luvluv	風
沙布日	sapuz	火
巴檸	banin	火塘
昆洪	gunhu	火炭
布蘇魯基斯	bulsuklukis	乾柴
凱里旺	qailivan	肉脯
乾旺	ganvan	水鹿
羅博	lutbu	身體
迪哈擰	dihanin	大自然

部落百寶盒：木刻畫曆

用漢字拼讀	布農語	漢語名詞
卡尼多岸社	Qanituan	卡尼多岸社（部落名）
塔魯姆・滿來旺	Talum mangdavan	塔魯姆・滿來旺（姓氏）

部落百寶盒：祭典豐富的布農族

用漢字拼讀	布農語	漢語名詞
柄都散	bintusan	成年禮
馬拉卡泰那	malaqtainga	打耳祭（又稱射耳祭）
卡奴布	qanup	祭典前的打獵
帕丁哈爾	patinqal	對空鳴槍傳訊息
馬丁帕斯度	matinpasdu	迎接獵人
比斯拉賀	pislahi	祭獵槍
馬巴非士	mapatvis	獵骨祭
馬巴那泰那	mapanaktainga	射耳
都虎米斯	tauqumis	祈求孩童成為英雄
馬巴希奴爾	mapaꞓitnul	分吃祭拜過的烤肉
馬拉斯達邦	malastapan	報戰功

部落百寶盒：天籟八部合音享譽國際

用漢字拼讀	布農語	漢語名詞
巴希布布	pasibutbut	小米豐收祈禱歌

部落百寶盒：布農族的分布與社會組織

用漢字拼讀	布農語	漢語名詞
達給督度	Takitudu	卓社群
達給巴哈	Takibakha	卡社群
達給娃旦	Takivatan	丹社群
達卡巴奴阿	Takbanuaz	巒社群
伊斯布滾	Isbukun	郡社群

 鄒 族

小筆記 ▶

・玉山的鄒語發音為「八通關」，是天神居住聖地。

・世居阿里山，20多年來成功復育達娜伊谷溪生態。

・備受推崇的音樂家、教育家高一生，曾任吳鳳鄉（已正名為阿里山鄉）鄉長，死於白色恐怖。

‧父系社會，親屬組織清楚分為家族、世系與氏族三層次

‧原本被稱為「南鄒」、世居高雄山區的拉阿魯哇族（Hla'alu）、卡那卡那富族
（Kanakanavu）於2014年6月正名。

故事導讀　人的團結與自然的界線

鄒族人口約七千多人，算是原住民各族中的小族群。但是他們人才濟濟，雄踞在阿里山，始終保持著他們獨特的民族風格。

因為巨鰻橫躺在河流下游的出口處，引發了大洪水。這次的災難，雖然最後只有鄒族人爬到玉山頂上，但族人人口的損失必定是十分慘重的。幸虧巨蟹的介入，化解了這次自然的災難。劫後餘生的族人最後整合為兩支，一支稱為「鄒」，另一支稱為「馬雅」，並以折箭為信物。「鄒」在阿里山特富野定居，「馬雅」則往日本方向遷移，竟不知所終。

洪水和馬雅人的失蹤，大概就是鄒族人口稀少的原因吧！可能也因為這個緣故，鄒族特別重視大社、小社間的連結和情感的維繫。「荷美雅雅」祭典時小社族人回到大社與分開的族人相聚，猶如回娘家，充滿歡樂的氣氛。而「休史吉」節慶，則是大社各氏族前往小社會見親屬，場面一樣熱烈。就在這樣大社、小社互訪的祭儀中，團結了整個鄒族。

在台灣原住民各族中，有關人和動物相戀的故事並不少。物類變形而感通，在泛靈信仰的傳統裡，並不是什麼稀奇的事。百步蛇變現人形與排灣公主相戀；鹿公子與卑南女子情深義重，終至以身相殉。諸如此類的故事，在各族口傳文學中並不陌生。然而，人獸之間，終究分屬不同的類別，有著各自的生活規範，因而這類的跨界行為，始終隱含著矛盾、悲劇的成分。〈復仇的山豬〉可能是台灣原住民各族這類故事中，最血腥、慘烈的一則。豬首領對美麗鄒族女子的愛慕，使牠越界變形，破壞人道與獸道的界線。愛情可以蒙蔽鄒族女子的眼睛，但無法躲過獵人哥哥執法的雙眼。事跡一旦敗露，一連串人獸間殲滅性的相互仇殺便展開了。鄒族人更少了，而被破壞的大地也使山豬日益減少。人和自然之間其實有著很深的矛盾、緊張關係，如何保持彼此的和諧與互惠？考驗著人類的智慧。

Reader's Guide   Bonds Among People; Boundaries of Nature

The Tsou's population is just over 7,000, which is considered to be a relatively small number among Taiwan's indigenous peoples. Despite the small number, they are considered exceptionally talented. They live primarily in and around Alishan, and have consistently maintained their unique ethnic style.

The giant eel, lying across the lower reaches of the river caused a great flood. In this disaster, although only the Tsou people made it to the top of Yushan Mountain, the losses to their population was catastrophic. Thanks to the giant crab's intervention, the disaster was resolved and the people who survived were integrated into two branches, one called "Tsou" and the other called "Maya", with the two parts of a broken arrows as the symbol of their bond. The Tsou settled in Tfuya on Alishan, while the Maya moved towards Japan, although no one knows where the Maya finally ended up.

The flood and the disappearance of the Maya are probably the reasons for the sparse population of the Tsou. Perhaps for these reasons the Tsou pay special attention to the connections between the large settlements and the small settlements. During the Homeyaya festival, the members of the small settlements return to the large settlements. It is as though they are returning to their mother's home, a joyful event. In the Siuski festival, the clans of the large settlements go to the small settlements to meet their relatives, and the scenes are just as enthusiastic. These ceremonies and mutual visits by the large and small settlements serves to unite all the members of the Tsou.

Among the indigenous peoples of Taiwan, it is not unusual for a story to narrate the love between humans and animals. Indeed, this is true for all animistic traditions, where great interspecies transformations occur. We have the Paiwan story about the Hundred Pace Snake that took on human form and fell in love with the princess; the Puyuma story about the deer and the Puyuma woman's a deep but sorrowful relation. Stories like this are not unfamiliar in the oral literature.

However, as between humans and other animals, they are after all different species with different standards for living, and thus this type of cross-species behavior inevitably implies contradictions and tragedies. The Tsou story of the Revenge of the Mountain Boar may be the bloodiest and most tragic of indigenous stories in Taiwan. The boar leader's adoration of the beautiful Tsou woman allowed it to transform and transcend the boundary between human and other animals. While love blinded the eyes of the Tsou woman, it could not prevent the eyes of her hunter brother from seeing what he perceived as a transgression.

Once the deeds were revealed, a series of annihilating mutual vendettas between humans and the mountain boar began. Both the populations of the Tsou people, and the wild boars were decimated, as were the lands ravaged by their warfare. Deep contradictions and tensions exist between humans and the rest of nature. Maintaining a harmonious and reciprocal relationship with nature is the true test of human wisdom.

01

折箭之約

歷經洪水而倖存的鄒族人，為了尋找心目中的樂土，決定各奔前程，於是忍住悲傷道別，折斷弓箭約定來日相見。

現在的鄒族老人，看到容貌和體格都酷似的日本人，不禁想起帶著另一半折箭離去的馬雅族人。馬雅族人在何方？請帶著折箭來相認吧！

很久以前，有一條身軀碩大的巨鰻，橫躺在河流下游出口處，堵塞了河道。

這條巨鰻一動也不動，使得積水無法消退，水勢日漸高漲，淹沒了群山。

於是，人們只好拼命往高處逃跑，但是水勢仍不斷上漲，最後只剩下鄒族人爬到玉山山頂。

這時候有一隻巨蟹，發現巨鰻橫躺不動，以為巨鰻早已死去，便用牠的螯用力夾住巨鰻的肚臍，巨鰻疼痛得翻身甩尾。

巨鰻這麼一動，才讓河道得以疏通，淤積已久的河水逐漸流入大海，汪洋一片的洪水因此慢慢消退，重現群山大地。

倖存的鄒族人經過這場洪水大災難後，彼此更加珍惜生命與患難之情的可貴，憑著樣貌、服飾、語言等特徵，很快地聚集了當初躲避洪水而分散在玉山山頂的族人，並建立了兩個社群。

 What's more?

群山：指玉山山脈，（Patungkuonu，八通關），因此也有人稱玉山為「八通關」，就是沿用此鄒語發音。玉山在鄒族人心目中是眾天神居住地、神聖的地方，天神也在此創造鄒族人。

特富野社（Tfuya）：是鄒族的大社之一，位在嘉義縣阿里山鄉達邦村一帶。鄒族的大社還有達邦社、魯富都社、沙阿魯阿社、卡那卡那夫社。

特富野社和達邦社是北鄒僅剩的二個大社，而在地理位置上位於這兩個大社的南邊，也就是現在嘉義縣山美、新美、茶山三個村的鄒族人，因為語言不同，稱為南鄒；但是一般學術上所劃分的南鄒，指的是高雄縣三民鄉一帶的沙阿魯阿社及卡那卡那夫社。

其中一支稱為「鄒」，前往現在阿里山的特富野社定居；另一支稱為「馬雅」，則移居到遠在台灣北邊的日本。

他們在道別時將弓箭折成兩段，一半由前往特富野社方向的族群保留，另一半折箭交給了往日本方向的馬雅族群，做為日後相認的憑證。

當時帶領較多的族人往日本方向走的馬雅族群，最後卻所剩無幾，究竟是什麼原因，至今仍不得而知。

直到今天，鄒族人仍然稱呼日本人為「馬雅」，有別於其他原住民對日本人的稱呼，也許是因為懷念擁有另一半折箭的真正馬雅人，而將這種感情移轉在日本人身上吧！

現在還常聽到鄒族老一輩的人說，日本人剛來台灣時，由於長相和鄒族人輪廓神似，族人一度以為日本人就是失散好幾世紀的馬雅人。但是，初見面寒喧交談，卻發現彼此的語言無法溝通，服裝也大不相同，更沒有見到折箭信物，難以相認。

一直到今天，馬雅人故事成謎，也很難找到關於馬雅人的蛛絲馬跡。

Where did it come from?

本故事採集自嘉義縣阿里山鄉來吉村，由兩位年約80歲的耆老陳庄次、石英雄講述。

What's more?

鄒族人輪廓特徵：鄒族人長得中等身材、鼻挺、眼眉黑亮。

02

復仇的山豬

喜歡鄒族美麗女子的山豬首領，在夜裡幻化成英俊男子，與女子相戀，卻被女子的哥哥一箭射死。

失去首領的山豬群狂亂攻擊族人，殺了所有社裡的族人。外出打獵的男子們逃過一劫，合力為族人復仇，殺了山豬撫慰死去的族人，從此，山豬的數量就減少了。

在鄒族中流傳著一個故事，據說曾有一隻山豬化為非常英俊的男子，結識了社裡一位年輕漂亮的未婚女子。

這隻山豬白天常在社周圍的山林裡遊走，自從喜歡上這名年輕女子之後，便一直跟在她的身後，以愛慕眼光注視著她，片刻也不願離開。

到了晚上，山豬搖身一變，化為人形，藉故製造各種機會和年輕女子相遇、聊天。

由於山豬的積極和主動，年輕女子日漸被山豬吸引，兩人的感情進展快速，痴情的山豬已經可以大大方方到年輕女子家中做客，甚至留宿過夜呢！

他們交往了很長的一段時間，這位年輕女子從來都沒有發現她的情郎其實是一隻山豬。

後來，年輕女子開始感到疑惑：

「為什麼他只有在晚上的時候才出現，一到早上就看不見人影呢？」

有天晚上，年輕女子的哥哥因為白天打獵毫無所獲，失望地回家，途中恰巧發現一隻山豬正在社的出入口徘徊。女子的哥哥立刻精神大作，緊緊跟隨在山豬後面，準備伺機射殺。

What's more?

社：故事中的社，指的是（takupuyanou，達古布亞奴），這個族群已經滅社了，目前並無文獻記載。

這時，山豬在女子住家附近停住腳步，當女子的哥哥拿起弓箭準備射殺山豬時，令他錯愕的事情發生了！

那隻山豬竟在瞬間化作人形，從容不迫地進入他妹妹的房間裡。年輕女子的哥哥感覺到情況不妙，便守候在家門口附近，等著妹妹的情人出來。

果然，妹妹的情人走出自己家門口時又變回了山豬，哥哥立刻使用銳利的長矛把牠刺死。

年輕女子聽到了山豬的哀嚎聲，跑出來一看，才驚覺原來自己深愛的情人竟是山豬變成的，沒想到當初恩愛、甜美的時光，就在這一瞬間產生巨大的改變，也帶來慘烈後果。

這隻被殺死的山豬，正是附近山林裡所有山豬群的首領。

當山豬們察覺到首領一去不回後，知道必定遭到人類的無情獵殺了，於是瘋狂展開復仇行動。

山林裡成千上萬隻的山豬開始聚集，一群群快速奔跑到年輕女子居住的聚落，來勢洶洶，非常嚇人。

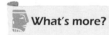

What's more?

男子會所（Kuba，庫巴）：會所的建築材料多就地取材，以木材建構及黃藤綁牢互相銜接而成，屋頂則以大量茅草層層覆蓋，整體建築形式離地約1.5公尺。會所為多功能之建築物，舉凡祭儀、訓練、會議等，都在此舉行。男子會所只有男子得以進入。

召開會議：通常由各家族長者代表。

勇士（Maotano，毛大諾）：成為勇士的條件是必須要與山豬搏鬥過，且是和已長出獠牙的山豬搏鬥。

社裡的人們一聽到山林中不斷傳來山豬群不尋常的咆哮聲，感到非常不安，直覺認為將有一大群的山豬來襲擊。

於是，他們便緊急到男子會所，召開會議共商抵禦山豬的對策。沒多久，社的入口塵土飛揚，山豬群奔騰攻擊過來了。

幸好男子會所的支柱很高，山豬沒有辦法爬上來，牠們只好在會所底下四處奔走騰躍、咆哮怒吼，而聚集在會所上的勇士們便拿起弓箭，射殺從四面八方攻來的山豬。

 What's more?

亞馬西亞那（yamasiana）：地名，位於現在的高雄縣境的楠梓仙溪流域一帶。

燒獵火攻（Phomeo，破米有）：燒獵的方式是以獵物群聚出沒的地區為主要範圍，掌握風向即開始由上風處焚燒，獵人及獵狗則在下風處守候獵捕。

勇士們的弓箭都射完了，但是山豬群的攻勢還是依然猛烈，最後勇士們只能以長矛，近距離刺殺山豬群，雖然每個人都筋疲力竭，但為了保衛族人和家園，仍奮力抵禦。

沒多久，被勇士們射殺而死的山豬屍堆已經堆到跟會所平台一樣高了，情況變得相當危急。

就在會所內的勇士們及所有人都還來不及應變的時候，山豬群踏過被殺死的山豬屍堆攻上會所，用牠們銳利的獠牙瘋狂地朝向人群刺殺。

不一會兒，山豬便把會所內所有的人殺死了，山豬群也慢慢離開。

當社遭到山豬攻擊時，社裡有一些獵人正在亞馬西亞那山區打獵。當他們高興地揹著獵物返家時，卻不見族人像往常一樣的歡喜迎接，反而異常安靜，心裡感到一定有不尋常的事發生。

直到獵人們到達會所，看見族人橫屍佈滿會所上下周圍，怵目驚心的景象令人難過。他們雖然逃過此劫，但卻恨不得能和族人同生共死。

忍住悲痛的情緒，獵人們理智地研判社裡凌亂的情景，發現族人遭受了山豬大規模的凌厲攻擊。

獵人們對於山豬近乎滅社的攻擊行徑非常憤怒，決心消滅所有山豬，誓死進行報復。

一行人當下決定立即出發，循著山豬的足跡，日夜趕路追蹤。

獵人們雖然發現山豬群停留的地點，但山豬數量實在太多，為避免寡不敵眾，居於劣勢，他們決定以平時打獵用的燒獵火攻來圍攻山豬。

在獵人們還沒來得及行動時，山豬群又開始大量移動，遷往別的地方。獵人們緊緊跟蹤，並推算山豬群應該正要前往亞古尤雜拿山的大草原，一夥獵人急速超前，先到那裡準備燒獵火攻需要的火料。

趁著山豬群剛到達亞古尤雜拿山，還一片紛亂的時候，獵人們點燃山豬群周圍乾燥的草原，火舌瞬間猛烈地從四周竄出蔓延，所有的山豬無所遁逃，全都陷在火海之中，陣陣淒厲尖銳的哀嚎聲不斷。

一段時間之後，火勢漸漸變小，大草原成了黑色灰燼，仍然輕飄著的煙霧，隨風緩緩地飄向遠方的部落，好像在撫慰那些死去的族人的靈魂，山林總算又恢復了寧靜。

聽說從那時起，山豬的數量就明顯減少了。

Where did it come from?
本故事由作者整理耆老口述而成。

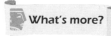
What's more?

亞古尤雜拿山（'akuingana）：語意是「螢火蟲的故鄉」，位於今嘉義縣阿里山鄉里佳村。

火料（popsusa，波布波司撒）：材料為乾燥的木屑。

被遺忘的祭典

> 每當鄒族新年「荷美雅雅」祭典來臨時，小社族人回到大社參加；而「休史吉」祭典則是大社族人來到小社接受款待。
>
> 這兩個祭典象徵著鄒族大、小社之間文化命脈的連結。鄒族的傳統祭典，讓感恩、不忘本的心意長存，也凝聚了族人情誼。

大社和小社

來吉村位於嘉義縣阿里山鄉北邊，東依塔山之下，塔山，是鄒族人傳說中的聖山，也是鄒族人死後靈魂的歸宿。從來吉村仰視塔山，昂然矗立的雄偉山勢，令人震懾於神秘的威嚴，又好像一位堅守崗位的衛兵，永遠守護著鄒族人的生命與繁衍。

▶ 狩獵屋逐漸發展成為「小社」

來吉這個小社是當初特富野大社族人狩獵處形成的聚落，成立到現在，至少有二百年了。為什麼會有大社、小社呢？

狩獵是從前鄒族人賴以維生的生活模式，起初，從大社出發，如果順利打到獵物，便可以當天返回大社。但隨著動物遷移路線的變動，獵場領域慢

What's more?

大社：在鄒族人的認知上，「社」應該有聚落型態、男子會所，以及自己的獵場（領域），並舉行各項重要祭儀，例如特富野社、達邦社。

來吉村（lalaci，拉拉吉）：指現在的嘉義縣阿里山鄉來吉村。

阿里山（soseongana，蒐朽嘎那）：意思是有很多松樹或檜木生長的地方，不過在日治時期，許多松樹或檜木林已經被砍伐另做他用了，取而代之的是人工植林。現在僅存的台灣原生林相，希望大家共同維護。

狩獵：對鄒族人而言，狩獵是嚴肅神聖的，狩獵之前要先夢卜、祭拜山神以保佑狩獵平安與豐收。

獵場（hupa，乎巴）：鄒族獵場（狩獵區）以各氏族來劃分，等於是家族的生存空間、領域，也是鞏固家族關係的表現。各獵場禁止他人任意進出、使用。

狩獵屋（hnou，和諾摩）：狩獵屋的建材沒有特定的材料，都以當地可以隨手取得的材料建置。

慢由近向遠擴展，所以打獵的範圍越來越大，路途也越來越遙遠，獵人們逐漸無法當天往返。因此，獵人們會在打獵的路途中搭建簡易的狩獵屋，作為夜宿休息的場所。

後來，常常出外到遙遠獵場打獵的獵人，為了解決思念親人之苦，於是帶著家人搬到狩獵屋，方便全家人一起生活。

當獵人們覺得狩獵屋附近是很適合居住的地方，就乾脆把全家人和家當搬遷過來定居；經過一段時間之後，搬遷過來定居的獵人越來越多，便漸漸形成新的「聚落」，就稱為「小社」。來吉村在發展成小社後，從最早五個氏族遷居過來，到現在已經增加到十二個氏族。

▶ 重要祭典都回到「大社」舉行

住在小社的獵人雖然離開大社，組成新的聚落，但仍時常掛念大社的一切，每年都會定期回去，從不間斷。

過去鄒族社會結構是以「大社」為主，也就是說，鄒族所有的重要祭典、節慶都是在大社舉行。

由於來吉社是從特富野大社分出來的，所以一直謹守著「以特富野大社為中心」的訓示，每當大社有節慶或有重要事情需要討論，小社的族人會以一個家族為單位，分別回到特富野大社，參加所屬的氏族活動。

What's more?

定期回去：遇到鄒族主要的祭典，如荷美雅雅、馬雅士比（mayasvi；鄒族傳統的戰祭，主要感謝天神昔日庇佑，並祈求來年戰事順利）等祭典，以大社為舉行的單位，與整個家族有關，小社的族人就必須回大社參加。

有關鄒族氏族繁衍、親屬關係，以及大社與小社的關係請參見「部落百寶盒」之「鄒族的社會組織」。

「荷美雅雅」節慶：小社回到大社

大社的傳統祭典，到今天仍有許多被保留、傳承下來，但是，屬於小社的祭典，卻因時代的變遷、鄒族社會組織改變等因素，漸漸地被遺忘，而「休史吉」就是其中之一。

什麼是「休史吉」呢？要了解這個傳承已久的風俗，就必須先從「荷美雅雅」節慶談起。

住在小社的族人每年定期回到大社與家族親屬相聚時，會詳細報告新聚落的生活情形，讓大社族人了解；若捕獲豐富的獵物，也會帶回大社與族人分享。

每次回大社，就彷彿漢民族農曆過年「回娘家」的情形，充滿歡樂的氣氛，而這種家族相聚的活動，鄒族人稱之為「荷美雅雅」。

所以，當「荷美雅雅」節慶來臨時，小社（或聚落）所有家族都會回到大社與分開的族人相聚，而停留在大社的時間則沒有硬性的規定。

 What's more?

鄒族的傳統祭典，請參見「部落百寶盒：鄒族傳統祭典（上）、（下）」。

社會組織改變：鄒族原有的大、小社的社會組織，在日治時代被日本人重新劃分行政區域而打散了，傳統祭典儀式從此也漸漸被遺忘。另外，這幾十年來漢人文化的傳入，更加速傳統祭典的消失。

休史吉（siuski）：語意為「回請」、「回應」。休史吉節慶主要在凝聚家族間的情感和共識，對於鄒族社會結構的維護，以及傳統文化的保存有正面幫助。在許多人奔走之下，停辦60年的休史吉祭典，在2001年5月5日首次於嘉義縣阿里山鄉來吉部落再度舉辦。休史吉祭典請參見「部落百寶盒：鄒族傳統祭典（上）」。

荷美雅雅（homeyaya）：在小米成熟時節7、8月間所舉行的祭典，又稱小米收穫祭，鄒族人會在這時祭祀小米神。請參見「部落百寶盒：鄒族傳統祭典（上）」。

「休史吉」節慶：大社探望小社

休史吉正好和荷美雅雅相反，是大社各氏家族前往小社會見親屬。休史吉節慶的前幾天，小社族人會總動員清除社內道路兩邊的雜草，以示歡迎遠道而來的親族；同時各家族都會提早釀酒以招待訪客。

▶ 各氏族的大小社家族團聚

休史吉節慶當天一早，小社長老用清晰又宏亮的歡呼催促聲，劃破原本寧靜的清晨，揭開當天活動的序幕。

族人在社裡穿梭來往，從這家族被邀請到另一家族，每個都顯得非常忙碌，處處洋溢著歡樂的氣息。不一會兒，社裡各處炊煙輕飄，夾雜著山豬的哀嚎聲，雖然聽來刺耳，但卻代表著各氏家族團聚，即將共享美食好酒的節慶前奏。

上午大約十點，大社的親族陸續抵達小社，社裡廣場已經聚集了穿著鮮紅傳統服飾的族人，儀式即將展開。這時，大社頭目、長老及各家族代表的男性都到齊了，一起步行前往距離聚落約一公里的入口處。

到了之後，族人會先種植象徵鄒族的神樹赤榕，並設置巴摩門特，召喚守護

What's more?

歡呼催促聲：意思是，來吧！讓我們開始來舉行慶典。

十點：昔日鄒族人以太陽的位置判別時間，以現在二十四小時劃分為三、六、九、十二四個時刻，但對每個時刻沒有特定的詞，反而以當時自然現象或太陽的位置來形容當時的時刻，例如凌晨三點為「下露水」、凌晨六點是「早上」、早上九點為「中午之前的太陽」、中午十二點是「中午」、下午三點稱「太陽準備下山」、下午六點為「天黑」等等。

鮮紅傳統服飾：鄒族對於顏色並沒有特別的意義，但以紅色來說，大部分表示好事。

神降臨。神樹赤榕一定要種在聚落的出入口處，因為天神會附身在神樹上。

當神樹赤榕和巴摩門特都安置完成，代表鄒族的社或部落正式成立，休史吉節慶就此揭開序幕。

一切準備就緒，頭目一聲號令指示，族人們手牽著手，圍繞在神樹四周，開始吟唱「迎神曲」。吟唱的儀式進行告一段落後，全體又回到社裡，繼續進行下一個活動。

▶ 安、鄭、武、洋姓氏不可互相嫁娶

接下來是家族相聚時刻，小社族人邀請同一氏家族的大社族人來訪，主要目的是讓家族的下一代子女認識親族關係，特別是傳統氏族觀念中，同氏族的人不可以互相嫁娶。

像是漢姓中的安、鄭、武、洋不可相互嫁娶，因為這四個姓氏在鄒族的傳統氏族制度上是同源於亞細憂古氏族，其他姓氏也同樣有如此的關係。

另外，長老們也藉著家族大團聚，對年輕一代口述家族遷移的歷史，甚至整個部落的建立過程。

休史吉節慶活動特別注重大社和小社之間的互動，一直是鄒族重要的傳統文化活動，如今卻因為時代變遷而疏於延續，已經漸漸被現存的鄒族人所遺忘。

Where did it come from?

本故事為採集者參與2001年來吉社區發展協會復辦休史吉祭典籌備會議中，請耆老口述經整理而成。

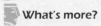 **What's more?**

赤榕（yono，右諾）：鄒族神話相傳天神搖晃赤榕樹，掉下來的葉子便成了鄒族人，赤榕與鄒族的起源息息相關，被稱為神樹，也被稱為生命之樹。

巴摩門特（Pa'momutu）：鄒族人在聚落的主要入口處，舉行簡單隆重的儀式設置巴摩門特，招喚天神降臨守護族人，其象徵意義如同漢人文化中的土地公，也如同設在軍營大門的檢查站。

迎神曲（ehoi，耶和伊）：即「歌的前言」之意。迎神曲的歌詞使用鄒族古語，鄒族人會唱，但歌曲意義目前僅能靠長老們來詮釋。

亞細憂古（yasiungu）：安氏族，請參見「部落百寶盒」之「鄒族的社會組織」。

部落百寶盒 ｜｜ 傳授哈「原」秘笈，搖身變成鄒族通

一、鄒族哲人高一生

高一生（Uongu Yatauyogana，吾壅·雅達烏猶卡那），1908年出生，天資聰穎。他是思想家、教育家與音樂家，可說是鄒族的菁英份子。他一生致力改善鄒族人生活，更以詩歌記錄鄒族文化與當時台灣發展的狀況。

▶ 鄒族現代化的第一推手

日治時代高一生接受師範教育，畢業後回阿里山達邦教育所教書，兼達邦警察駐在所巡查。他是帶領鄒族人現代化的第一人，對於鄒族的教育相當重視，鼓勵鄒族子弟接受新式教育。在同時他也協助日本統治者進行「理番」工作，協助引進水稻技術、其他經濟作物的種植等。

二次大戰結束不久，高一生被國民政府任命為第一任阿里山鄉鄉長（當時為吳鳳鄉），繼續協助族人改善生活、建設地方，後因二二八事件受冤屈被捕，不久即遭槍決，當時他才46歲。近年來二二八解禁，許多冤屈得雪，高一生也是。2001年2月，嘉義市二二八紀念館舉辦高一生生平展，可說是正式為高一生平反。

▶ 音樂創作　撫慰俱疲的身心

高一生也是一位音樂創作家，創作過許多鄒族生活歌謠，至今仍流傳於部落間。入獄後的高一生也以音樂和妻子相互勉勵，以日本春神「春之佐保姬」的名字創作兩首歌曲給妻子，作為二人相互安慰的精神憑藉。

「春之佐保姬」帶給處於困頓的環境與身心俱疲的人希望與安慰，歌曲積極、充滿希望。這首歌歌詞由日語寫成，意思是：

是誰在呼喚，

在茂密的林野間，

在安靜的黎明中宛如銀色鈴鐺般的美麗聲音，

在呼喚著誰呢？

啊，

佐保姬，

春之女神啊！

目前市面上有以「春之佐保姬」為名的紀念專輯，專輯中的歌曲都是出自高一生手筆，歌詞以鄒語居多，其次日語和漢語。

欲參觀嘉義市二二八紀念館，請電洽：05-2786228　地址：嘉義市大雅路二段695號。

二、鄒族的社會組織

鄒族是一個父系社會，並且由親屬組織構成部落與政治權利的運作。親屬組織層次清楚，大致可分為家族、世系群族與氏族三個層次。

▶ 家族

由一個家屋和從這個家屋分出的成員所組成。

▶ 氏系群族

是構成鄒族社會的基本單位，同世系群的族人共有禁忌之屋、獸骨架，亦共有獵場、漁區與耕地。氏系群也是舉行小米收穫祭的單位，同一氏族的人互不通婚，同一個家族的人要守同一個禁忌。

禁忌之屋內部有一個底部圓形、縮口的古土器，用在祭典中炊食供奉祖靈的祭品，平時懸掛在頭目家的禁忌之屋中，不准以手觸之。

▶ 氏族

由世系群組成的更大親屬團體稱為氏族，氏族中最早確立的本支稱為「本家」，也以此為氏族名，氏族間除了血緣關係外，也包括領養、分家的後代。例如亞細憂古氏（yasiungu）中包括安家（yasiungu）、自安家分出的武家（muknana）、安氏的養子鄭家（tiaki'ana）、以及yasakiei家、teneoana家等。同一氏族的人共有獵場、漁區與耕地，但不能通婚。

鄒族各家族採集體居住方式，一個鄒族的完整部落包括大社以及從大社分出去的小社。

▶ 大社

約由十數戶家戶組成，再由數個聚落組成一個政治社會單位，有最重要的象徵——男子會所（註），並具有宗教與經濟上的權力。

▶ 小社

原本只是族人暫居之地，非久居，因此經濟、政治、宗教活動仍集中於大社。小社並無舉行重要祭典儀式的權力，與整個家族有關的小米收穫祭，或與整個部落有關的戰祭，都必須回到大社參加。

另外，鄒族部落的社會角色有頭目、軍事領袖、巫師、長老。

▶ 頭目

頭目是大社的領導人，由各氏系群中選出，被賦予極大的權力，負責部落內、外各項事物，但不包括軍事戰鬥的領導權。

▶ 軍事領袖

軍事權由稱為「征帥」的軍事領袖擁有，軍事領袖必須先成為勇士，並擁有許多的戰爭經驗與功績。

▶ 巫師

鄒族社會中還有巫師的角色，他們是人界與超自然世界的中介人物，能治病、占卜、預言、祈禱。

▶ 長老

世系群與氏族中具有領導地位的人被稱為長老，通常由族人中富有才幹與通曉族裡或社中事物者擔任，有權代表他的世系群出席部落的長老會議與主持宗教儀式。

註：「男子會所」（kuba，庫巴）。會所的建築材料多就地取材，以木材建構及黃藤綁牢、互相銜接而成，屋頂則以大量茅草層層覆蓋，整體建築離地約1.5公尺。會所為多功能之建築物，舉凡祭儀、訓練、會議等，都在此舉行。男子會所只有男子得以進入。

三、鄒族傳統祭典：小米收穫祭、休史吉祭與貝神祭

鄒族的祭典最為人熟知的，除了戰祭與小米收穫祭外，還有近幾年才恢復辦理的休史吉祭典，以及南鄒特有的貝神祭，以下分別敘述：

▶ 小米收穫祭

鄒族稱小米收穫祭為荷美雅雅（homeyaya）。鄒族以小米播種為一年的開始，以小米的收成為結束。小米成熟時節在7、8月間，這也是舉行小米收穫祭的時間，意義上如同漢人的「過年」，象徵著送別舊歲，迎接新的一年。

祭典以同姓氏的家族為單位，也就是氏系群，由家族的家長主祭，在家內的禁忌之屋舉行。這時居住在小社的同姓氏家族成員都會回到大社來參與。祭典的意義在慶祝豐收，並感念小米女神的恩賜，更藉著祭典強化家族的凝聚力。

小米收穫祭為期約15天，也可長達一個月，祭典期間族人必須禁食鹽、魚肉、蕃薯、薑、蒜等食物；其他禁忌還有摘下粟米時禁止與他人交談，禁止採柴薪與耕作等，若觸犯禁忌，來年家中的作物將無法豐收。

小米收穫祭結束後，各世系群的領導人會聚集在部落首長家族的禁忌之屋內，討論今年的戰祭是否舉行。

由於生態環境的改變，尤其是水稻傳入後，小米儀式及相關儀式漸漸產生變化。部落大、小社的關係也因新的行政區劃分而產生若干變化，使得現今儀式愈來愈簡略了。

▶ 休史吉祭典

鄒族舉辦小米收穫祭時，居住於小社的族人會回到大社參加慶典，在大社接受盛宴款待之後一週到兩週內，小社族人會邀請大社族人到小社接受盛宴招待，藉以連絡大、小社族人間的感情，這樣的活動就叫「休史吉」（siuski）。

鄒族的休史吉是小社對大社感恩回饋的一種儀式，面對時代變遷，導致傳統祭典被遺忘，各氏族之間的關係也愈來愈疏離的今天，休史吉祭典正可凝聚族人的情感。

▶ 貝神祭

貝神祭是南鄒族高雄縣桃源鄉沙阿魯阿社特有的祭典，顧名思義就是祭拜貝神。

相傳鄒族人發源於「拉蘇納」這個地方，當時與一群小矮人同住，後來為了求得更好的生存空間，準備遷往他處；離去時，與鄒族人相處融洽的小矮人特別送上最珍惜的12顆貝殼。據說，這些貝殼可以帶來豐收、健康、聰明、勇猛等12種好運，鄒族人於是妥善珍藏，平日都封存在一只甕裡，埋在頭目家後院。

貝神祭每2年舉行一次，祈求貝神降福族人。不久前，貝神祭在高雄重現，高雄縣桃源鄉由族中的長老帶著公主，將12顆珍藏的貝殼拋向天空，由勇士爭相撿取，象徵帶給族人勇猛、聰明等各種好運。

四、鄒族傳統祭典：戰祭

戰祭的鄒族語為馬雅士比（mayasvi），是個屬於整個部落的祭典，由大社主辦舉行，主要祭拜戰神，舉行的時間是每年2月15日或8月15日。由頭目或軍事領袖帶領，在部落內的男子會所進行，重點在於迎接天神、除舊佈新，除了感念以往戰事順利，也祈求來年的戰事都順利。

戰祭的過程有準備活動，以及迎神祭、團結祭、送神祭等三大主要儀式，另有路祭、家祭，還有歌舞祭與結束祭。

戰祭的準備活動首先是部落長老決議是否舉行？決議的時間在每年小米收穫祭時，若決定舉行，各氏族便立即開始準備祭品、準備修建會所用的茅草、練習祭歌、通知小社族人回到大社參與祭典、整理祭屋與祭典環境。接著，族裡的男士開始修建會所屋頂，修建後，勇士穿著登會所裝進入會所，並配戴神花——木檞蘭在帽子上、繫避邪簽條在胸前，完成迎神準備，長老也在會所內勉勵勇士們。

▶ 迎神祭

戰祭的主要儀式首先是迎神祭，鄒勇士將代表戰神之火，同時也是代表生命的聖火移到祭典廣場中央，在赤榕神樹前殺乳豬祭神，並舉起沾血的刀向戰神呼嘯。接著砍神樹樹枝代表為戰神修築通往上天的天梯，然後留下三枝樹枝分別朝向其他部落會所。此時勇士們唱迎神曲迎接戰神降臨會所，唱完之後鄒勇士返回會所，此時戰神也已降臨會所。

▶ 團結祭

戰神降臨會所後，各氏族從祭屋取出酒、米糰等，先向戰神奠酒祝神，再把酒和米糰摻和後，請鄒勇士們共同飲食，以表示部落的團結。

之後，部落滿周歲的男嬰由母親抱著，到會所舉行男嬰初登會所禮，男嬰由他的舅舅抱上會所，親人向戰神奠酒祈祝，讓戰神認識這名男嬰，並由部落長老祝福男嬰成為勇士。

接著由氏族長老敘述英勇戰功，進行誇功禮，鄒勇士則全體複誦，結束時頓足踏地，砥礪族人士氣。

接近二十歲的成年男子也要在這個時候舉行成年禮，他們登上男子會所，蹲坐在長老前接受訓誡與勉勵，接著以藤條鞭打他們的臀部，再賜與皮帽、粟酒。這些男子此後就必須負起保護部落的責任，也開始擁有社會地位。

▶ 送神祭

成年禮結束後，鄒族勇士在廣場以舞隊、唱兩遍送神曲，送戰神升天。之後

改唱慢板戰歌，開始歌舞祭。此時婦女手持火把加入歌舞祭行列，並將火把放入廣場火堆中，代表部落農作之火與戰神之火合而為一。

在主要的祭典儀式結束後，鄒族勇士們一起步出會所，再前往部落征戰的道路舉行路祭，祈求征戰平安，路祭結束後，各氏族成員還必須準備米酒進行家祭。

到了夜晚，由長老帶領再次舉行歌舞祭，族人圍繞在祭典廣場火堆，以歌舞歌頌戰神。最後在午夜時刻由鄒勇士登上會所，再唱迎神曲、送神曲和戰歌，祭司向戰神唸誦，報告祭典已全部結束，廣場的火就可以熄滅。

目前戰祭儀式過程已大為簡化，僅保留簡單的路祭、象徵性的敵首祭、初登會所和成年禮等，由達邦及特富野兩大社輪流辦理。

五、美麗的生態保育地：達娜伊谷

嘉義縣阿里山鄉是鄒族人數最多的地方，這裡除了大家耳熟能詳的阿里山風景，近幾年來達娜伊谷(tanayiku)也廣為人知。位於山美社區的達娜伊谷是一個未開發的處女地，鄒族人在達娜伊谷溪復育高山鯝魚，每年舉辦的「鯝魚節」更吸引社會大眾參加而聲名大噪。

依山而居的鄒族人以河川為部落的屏障，豐饒的河川資源更提供了部落生活的糧食，是部落重要的財產之一。鄒族人除了分配獵場供氏族狩獵外，也將河川分成區段供各氏族管理使用，部落成員不但要學習管理，對其他氏族的河區更要尊重，不可侵犯。

過去鄒族捕魚有一定的規範，是一種永續利用及分享河川資源的觀念，使各種生態資源得以維持自然與平衡。但在阿里山過度開發下，河川生態遭逢空前浩劫之際，居民開始鼓吹愛惜河川生態資源。

▶ 巡河護魚　讓河川生命永續

1989年山美居民成立「山美觀光發展委員會」，選定尚保持原始風貌的達娜伊谷溪及兩岸的原始森林，作為生態保育地區，嚴禁開發，同時通過達娜伊谷生態保育計劃，訂下村民自制公約。

居民為避免生態遭受破壞，自己組成社區巡邏隊，由社區十五歲以上、五十歲以下男性，以白天1人，夜間2人之巡邏方式，輪流擔任巡河護魚任務。

透過保育達娜伊谷生態的過程中，社區居民在無形中教育自己、下一代及他人，使得珍惜傳統河川文化的認知，深植村民心中。

▶ 生態保育的最佳範例

1995年「達娜伊谷自然生態公園」正式成立且對外開放，園區可以賞魚，也有其他特殊景觀，如鬼山古道、龍鳳峽谷、仙井瀑布、燕子崖等。達娜伊谷將營運所得由社區統一規劃運用，做為舉辦各類活動的基金。

如今，達娜伊谷的生態保育已經成為社區的觀光資源，又逐漸恢復鄒族固有的河川文化，族人樂於按照傳統規範使用河川，是達娜伊谷生態保育成功的基本因素。

參觀達娜伊谷請洽：山美社區發展協會　電話：05-2586994。

六、鄒族的塔山與死亡觀

對鄒族人來說，死亡只是身體失去功能、消逝，意味著本來附著在人身上的靈，從這個人的身體分離出來，但靈仍然存在。靈不同於人，不受鄒人歡迎，必須將靈趕到在阿里山鄉來吉村附近的塔山。神聖的塔山是鄒族人死後靈魂的歸宿，即「靈的會所」。

鄒族人看待死亡有老死、病死、戰死的「善終」，以及自殺、他殺、夭死、遭巫師詛咒而死的「惡死」。善死的人靈魂是善良的，不會害人，靈會前往大塔山；惡死的人靈魂變成幽靈，會作祟害人，歸到小塔山。

▶ 鄒族傳統葬禮

鄒族傳統的喪禮在屋內進行，遺體也是埋葬於屋內。善終的人病危時，親人會聚集在旁，臨終的老人會有一番勉勵或遺囑。接著親人將病人移到屋內，讓他躺在用月桃葉葉鞘編織成的蓆子上，再為他換上正式場合的服裝。

等到病人斷氣後，便使其成蹲踞的姿態，兩手抱膝，以三枝木棒支撐身體，男子用藤皮、女子用布帶縛緊。隨後族內男子便在室內挖掘墓穴，讓屍體坐於穴中，用土石掩埋後，便在墓穴上燒柴，讓地面乾燥，近親就在地面上就寢，藉以安慰死者。

▶ 趨靈儀式

埋葬後，喪家需服喪五天，這段期間內，家屬及近親會停止一切工作表示哀悼。接著由母族家的男子（通常是死者的舅舅），舉行驅靈儀式，將死者的靈逐出屋外。驅靈者以棍子、茅草、藜實（黃色，形狀如小米的植物狀）等物品當器具，敲擊牆壁，並喊著：「離開這個家，你已經死了！離開這個家，以後不要再回來了」，將靈趕走；之後再以茅草結、木炭和藜實放在門檻上，防止死靈再回來。整個儀式結束後，親友們在屋內聚餐，這時葬禮才算完成。

造訪部落　**部落藏寶圖，來挖鄒族寶**

看過了鄒族的神話與傳說故事，你是否感動於大、小社族人，以荷美雅雅祭典與休史吉祭典維繫家族情感的那份心？是否也想感受一下祭典的歡樂？

鄒族有北鄒（嘉義縣阿里山鄉與南投縣信義鄉一帶）與南鄒（高雄縣三民鄉一帶）之分，但還是以阿里山鄉為主要分布區。

阿里山的鄒族主要分布於達邦村、樂野村、來吉村、里家村、山美村、新美村、茶山村等七個行政區域，目前僅剩下兩個大社──特富野與達邦。現在，透過這份精心編製的「嘉義縣市文化、旅遊景點導覽圖」、「阿里山鄉鄒族文化導覽圖」，陪伴身歷其境，盡情挖掘部落文化寶藏，一窺鄒族的特殊文化，體驗「塔山」的神聖，以及感受家族相聚歡樂的祭典，保證不虛此行。

當然，造訪部落時不能錯過鄒族豐富的祭儀活動，像是每年7、8月間達邦與特富野大社會舉行小米收穫祭，小社則於每年小米收穫祭後一週到兩週內舉行休史吉祭典；戰祭則於每年2月15日或8月15日，由達邦與特富野輪流舉行，舉行與否由長老決定。

祭典詳細時間及地點請洽：

嘉義縣政府　電話：05-3620123　網址：http://www.cyhg.gov.tw/

阿里山鄉公所　電話：05-2511001

鄒族
文化導覽圖

族語開口說　　**入境隨俗的鄒語**

你好嗎？
Misu umnu?
米蘇 恩奴
你　好嗎

你好！
Yokeoasu!
由給由阿酥
健壯(的)你

請問貴姓大名？
Cuma na ongko su?
珠麻　那 翁戈　蘇
什麼　的 名字　你

巴穌亞
'a Pasuya.
阿 巴穌亞
是 巴穌亞

請問你住在哪裡？
Mo yonenu na emoo su?
麼　有捏奴 那 也麼 穌
(助詞)在　　哪裡 的家 你

我住在達邦社山美村
Mo　yone saviki'o　emoo'u.
麼　有矗 撒弗依其 歐 也麼 屋
(助詞)在　山美村 那　家 我的

這是什麼？
Cuma na eni?
珠麻　那 也尼
什麼　的 這個

這是我們鄒族的神樹赤榕。
Tsou yono cila p'ohkui　ci evi.
肉　有諾 幾拉 薄何古伊 幾 也弗伊
是　赤榕 用來 朝拜　　的 樹

你們午餐都吃什麼？
Cuma na lamu ana homo oahtu?
珠麻　那 拉木 阿拿 後麼 挖合督
什麼　的 你們 習慣 吃當 中餐

肉和地瓜。
'a fou ho fue
阿否　合 夫ㄟ
是肉　和 地瓜

你們的部落什麼時候舉行戰祭？
Homna　na lamu mayasvi?
厚們　　納 拉木 馬雅士比
什麼時候 那 你們 戰祭

我們的部落在2月15日舉行。
'a hola　　feohu no 'eosa
阿 和拉　夫有和 諾 也有撒
是 習慣在 月亮　的 第二

這是什麼魚？
Yosku Cuma na eni?
有司可 珠麻　那 也你
魚　　什麼　的 這個

他們是達娜伊谷特有的魚。
Tsou yosku ne tanaiku.
肉 有司可 聶　達娜伊谷
是 魚　　屬於 達娜伊谷

我們喜歡你們的部落。
Os'o　umnua'e hosa mu.
歐司歐 恩奴阿 耶 后撒 木
我　　很喜歡 這 部落 你們的

謝謝你的到來。
'aveoveoyu ho mimu esmmi.
阿弗友弗友 后 米木　耶司米
感謝　　　當 你們　來

很高興認識你。
Umnu ho mito yupa bohngu
恩奴　和 密多 幽巴 伯和奴
很好　當 我們 互相 認識見面

希望能再相見！
Tato'so la i'vaho yupa baito!
達多收 拉 一發和　幽巴 攔多
我們將期待再 一次 互相 見面

下次再見！
Tato'so　　la　i'vaho yupa baito!
達多收　　拉　一發和 幽巴 攔多
我們將期待 再　一次　互相 見面

歡迎下次再來。
Temu'so la i'vaho uh tan'e
爹木縮　拉 一發后 屋 但聶
希望你們 再 一次　來 這裡

鄒族發音說明：字母中常有「'」的發音，要發喉塞音。

學習加油站　**本書漢語與鄒語名詞對照表**

故事01：折箭之約

用漢字拼讀	鄒語	漢語名詞
篤佑莎	tungeoza	巨鰻
鄒	Tsou	鄒族人
眉諾攸果	meoi no yongo	巨蟹
不之古	pucku	肚臍
記夫記	civci	尾
督布	tupu	洪水
吉有瓦大和奔科	ceoa ta hpuhpungu	大地
亞諾速右	yaa no suyu	弓箭
馬雅	maya	日本
文莫沙	omza	北方
達伊放	taivan	台灣
密阿阿屋奴	mi'a'aunu	長相
也ㄟ	e'e	語言
亦益厚薩	'i'ihosa	服裝
呼窩翁西基麻住住麻	huomzi ci macucuma	信物

故事02：復仇的山豬

用漢字拼讀	鄒語	漢語名詞
耶後漢發	ehohangva	故事
夫出	fuzu	山豬
哈後子	haahocngu	男子
麻沒司必宜	maamespingi	女子
耶耶弗依	'e'evi	山林
伯和恩奴	buh'umnu	愛慕
麼宙	mcoo	眼
雅大地司歌拔	yatatiskova	人
耶摩	emoo	家
又夫那	yofna	晚上
密司及	miski	過夜
舟尼西	conisi	（他的）情人
達修拿	taseona	早上

歐海伊法	ohaeva	哥哥
歐海伊撒	ohaesa	妹妹
也麼	emoo	房子
披擬	phingi	門
舟尼屋	coni'u	（我的）情人
夫穌尤	fsuyu	長矛
尤若門	yuozomu	首領、頭目
司諾麼折剎	snomcoza	獵殺
杜木度木諾一	tmutmunoi	咆哮聲
偌大有	zotayo	襲擊
哈能	hangu	敵人
司耶司	suesu	支柱
酥攸末	suyumo	攻擊
索耶得扎	so'eut' uca	保衛
尼亞夫亞各	niafeango	屍
荷依西	hisi	獠牙
夫野窟	fuengu	山區
否屋	fou	獵物
阿多阿那	a'toana	族人
鄒扎泊後	cocaphu	足跡
阿蘇司卡	a'suska	報復
由諾恩	yun'u	草原
不若	puzu	火
郭阿俄喀	koa'onga	黑色
富	efuu	灰燼

故事03：被遺忘的祭典

用漢字拼讀	鄒語	漢語名詞
賀支本	hohcubu	塔山
麼哲伊	mcoi	死
和肉	hzoo	靈魂
貝西亞吉夫一庫	peisia ci fuengu	聖山
后撒	hosa	部落
壽	nsou	生命
亞否屋	yaa fou	打獵
憂瓦首	yuansou	動物
掠雅否屋	leyaafou	獵人

瓦橫	'oahngu	親人
歐憂那	'oyona	居住
諾耶如呼	noezuhu	搬遷
咩西	meesi	祭典
嗎斯斯得	mahsusuftu	訓示
周諾阿耶嗎那	cono aemana	家族
咩西諾補督	meesi no puutu	過年
補督	puutu	漢民族
磨崖也密	moyai emi	釀酒
吉有諾	ceonu	道路
固固若	Kukuzo	雜草
阿夫有夫有	'aveoveoyu	歡迎
麻米有宜	maameoi	長老
飛油飛油	feufeu	炊煙
業弗依諾黑住	evi no hicu	神樹
阿給麻木有一	ak'emameoi	守護神
歐歐格	'o'oko	子女
多橫個	'tohungu	情感
歐憂恩收發	h'oyunsova	文化

部落百寶盒：鄒族哲人高一生

用漢字拼讀	鄒語	漢語名詞
吾壅・雅達烏猶卡那	UonguYatauyogana	高一生

部落百寶盒：鄒族的社會組織

用漢字拼讀	鄒語	漢語名詞
亞細憂古	yasiungu	安氏族

部落百寶盒：鄒族傳統祭典：小米收穫祭、休史吉與貝神祭

用漢字拼讀	鄒語	漢語名詞
荷美雅雅	homeyaya	小米收穫祭
休史吉	siuski	回請、回應

部落百寶盒：鄒族傳統祭典：戰祭

用漢字拼讀	鄒語	漢語名詞
馬雅士比	mayasvi	戰祭

挑戰 Q&A

信心滿滿，泰雅、布農、鄒族
大小事輕鬆答！

▶ 泰雅族

1. 泰雅族祖先是從哪裡生出來的？位置在哪個縣市？

2. 在巨石傳說中，一共有幾個男女走出來，後來只剩下幾人？為什麼？

3. 泰雅族的紋面習俗流傳已久，請說出女性紋面習俗的由來？

4. 為什麼泰雅族人諄諄告誡後代，千萬不可以用手指著在天上高掛的七色彩虹？

5. 傳說中的彩虹橋是誰幻化而來的？他因為具備什麼條件，受人尊敬而成為精神領袖？

6. 泰雅族人相信他們死後都將經過彩虹橋的審判？請問什麼樣的人才可以順利走過彩虹？

7. 泰雅族人平日要遵守族人共同制定的規範，這個待人處事的生活紀律泰雅語要怎麼說？

8. 以前的泰雅族人怎麼呼喊山豬和木柴？

9. 以前的泰雅族人生活上所需要的東西有多方便？請列舉二種情形。

10. 這些生活上的方便讓泰雅族人吃用不愁，卻因為族人曾經做了什麼事而永遠失去了？請列舉二種。

▶ **布農族**

1. 「與月亮的約定」這篇故事裡，為什麼布農族父子要射下太陽？後來結果怎麼樣？

2. 布農族父子和月亮約定了些什麼？這些約定對於布農族的生命禮俗、歲時祭儀又有什麼影響？

3. 布農族女孩阿朵兒被阪達浪獵頭隊抓走後，有什麼遭遇？

4. 阿朵兒後來生了一個兒子，阪達浪人都叫他馬耀‧骨木爾，為什麼阿朵兒都叫他迪樣？迪樣為什麼都被欺負？

5. 阿朵兒為什麼教迪樣把小米藏起來？他們怎麼解決逃難中的困難？

6. 阿朵兒回到布農族部落後和丈夫團聚了嗎？後來怎麼了？

7. 迪樣長大後對布農族人有什麼貢獻？

8. 卡布斯幫丈夫編織衣服時，參考哪一種動物身上的花紋？

9. 布農族對百步蛇的有兩種稱謂，各是什麼？又各代表什麼意思？

10. 獵人們遇到颱風仍執意趕回部落，後來這些人怎麼了？讀完這則故事你有什麼心得？

▶ 鄒族

1. 請形容玉山在鄒族人心目中的地位；為什麼有人把玉山叫做「八通關」？

2. 鄒族在歷經洪水災難後建立了哪兩個族群？後來這兩個族群各自遷移到哪裡？他們約定日要怎麼相見？

3. 你知道鄒族人怎麼稱呼日本人嗎？為什麼鄒族老人看到日本人，感到特別熟悉與親切？

4. 喜歡鄒族年輕少女、能化成人形的山豬首領，是被誰揭穿身份的？下場如何？

5. 鄒族人在進行對山豬報復時，最後用什麼方法成功？

6. 鄒族的大社與小社有什麼關係？請說明大社和小社之間有什麼區別？

7. 鄒族重要的「荷美雅雅」與「休史吉」祭典是在什麼時候舉行？這些祭典有什麼傳統意義呢？

8. 鄒族的神樹是什麼？他們的守護神又是什麼？你能說說看神樹和守護神有什麼關係嗎？

9. 請說出「男子會所」在鄒族的社會中，有什麼重要的意義？又有什麼禁忌？

10. 這些發生在台灣遠古時代的神話與傳說故事，看完之後有什麼心得？

E 網 情 報 站

輕鬆上網搜尋，「原味」超靈通

這些團體默默耕耘，收集整理了有關原住民文化、原鄉風光等等豐富內容，值得上網共享：

1 雲裡的織布

花蓮縣新城鄉嘉里國小同學製作，介紹泰雅族織布，包括織布的材料、工具、樣式等，並有泰雅族的起源傳說、日常生活等資料。

2 山中傳奇一泰雅族

由苗栗育民工家同學所製作的網頁，介紹泰雅族的種族起源、文化語言、生活方式、年祭慶典、巫術占卜、神話傳說等，蒐集的資料內容非常豐富而詳實。

3 即將消逝的彩霞一泰雅紋面藝術

花蓮縣鑄強國小學生製作，介紹泰雅族文化歷史、紋面藝術之創作過程、形式及涵義、關懷紋面老人等。

4 飛鼠部落

行政院國科會科學教育處補助之專題研究計畫「飛鼠部落：泰雅族世界觀導向之科學學習活動網站開發與研究」之部分研究成果。內容包括神話、傳統音樂歌謠、泰雅族語發音、紋面臉譜、北德拉曼山神木群等原住民文化資訊。

5 新竹縣尖石鄉公所

位於新竹縣，提供人文風情、原住民泰雅族、風景、觀光、交通、母語教育、農業特產及造林等資訊，及那羅灣休閒農業區園區介紹。

6 花蓮縣豐濱鄉公所

豐濱鄉內原住民村落歷史、文化及景觀介紹。

7 泰雅渡假村網站

泰雅渡假村是一個全方位的多功能渡假村，其網站上亦有泰雅族歷來的文化與風俗習性介紹。

8　新竹縣原住民族教育資源中心

介紹泰雅族、賽夏族的禮俗慶典、遷徙源流、神話傳說、傳統飲食，並有五峰鄉、尖石鄉的觀光生活資訊。

9　飛魚雲豹音樂工團

以音樂作為原住民文化復興的媒介，演唱者包括泰雅族、泰雅族、卑南族、排灣族族等歌手

10　花蓮縣原住民族教育資原中心

花蓮縣原住民民族教育資源中心，積極推廣原住民民族課程和教學，蒐集及整理文物資訊，協助並支援關於原住民民族教學活動。

11　國立台灣史前文化博物館

以保存、研究卑南等重要遺址及其出土古文物的文化遺留為主，展示並致力推廣考古學、人類學等社會文化教育。

12　交通部光觀局花東縱谷國家風景管理處

一次飽覽台灣花東縱谷的綺麗風光及人文特色，並可了解當地的光觀資源、遊憩據點、旅遊資訊，還有貼心的旅程安排等資訊。

13　布農尋根之旅全球資訊網

花蓮縣萬榮鄉馬遠國小學生參加2001年台灣學校網界博覽會所製作的專題網站。網站內整理許多布農族文化資訊，相當值得參考。

14　高雄市政府文化局

蒐集高雄縣境內六大族群傳統歌謠，並提供MP3下載。

15　布農文教基金會

1998年成立於台東延平鄉桃源村的布農文教基金會，是一個由原住民成立的公益基金會，網站內有基金會推動部落重建工作內容、台東布農部落介紹、藝文活動資訊等等。

16　花蓮縣社區總體營造資訊網・古風社區

記錄花蓮縣卓溪鄉的古風社區如何發展屬於自己的布農社區文化，如果想了解古風社區的布農文化，這個網站是一定要瀏覽的。

17 **高雄市原住民局**
內有高雄市內原住民鄉鎮文化、活動介紹。

18 **行政院原住民委員會／原住民族資訊網**
舉凡原住民權益、法規、族群及文化介紹等等，十分豐富。

19 **原住民族委員會原住民族文化發展中心**
有原住民園區風采介紹、山海的精靈（原住民介紹）、原鄉藝文、
兒童園地、母語教室等，相當值得流覽。

20 **公共電視原住民新聞雜誌**
提供有關原住民新聞、活動訊息、原住民資料庫。

21 **台北市政府原住民事務委員會**
介紹原住民各族群及原住民音樂等，並呈現歷年來台北原住民文化
祭活動內容。

22 **原住民族歷史與社會議題教學資源網站**
由台北市教育局委製，分生活、文化、歷史掌故、神話篇，介紹原
住民文化，還有原住民學習單下載及線上即時測驗。

23 **九族文化村－原住民文化**
網頁中有原住民文化介紹、部落景觀、歷史照片、音樂，以及傳統
手工藝的概述。

24 **原舞者**
原住民藉由歌曲及舞蹈將傳統文化、歷史代代相傳，因此「原舞
者」致力於將原住民歌舞藝術推廣傳承，更希望走向世界。

25 **山海文化雜誌社**
以維護並發展原住民文化、促進社會對原住民的了解與尊重為宗
旨；網站提供協會簡介與消息、山海出版社出版資訊。

26　嘎拉賀楓林農場

提供住宿及行程規劃服務，內有攝影日記、沿途景點、泰雅族部落介紹等。

27　順益台灣原住民博物館

館內主要蒐藏、研究並展示台灣原住民文物，藉教育活動之推廣來呈現台灣本土文化之樣貌。

28　高屏原住民文化采風

由劉嘉雄老師所設計的鄉土補充教材。包含台灣原住民族群分布與文化特色，及原住民文化采風。

29　幸福綠光股份有限公司

【台灣原住民的神話與傳說】透過生動的故事，搭配精緻彩繪圖畫，勾勒出原住民信仰、儀式、禁忌、圖騰、生活智慧與技能，並透過中 、英文對照，希望讓國人以及海外讀者能認識台灣原住民寶貴的生活文化遺產，也讓台灣這段遠古歷史變得清晰、鮮活、可親。

泰雅族
Atayal

01

The Legend of the Giant Stone

> One day long ago, touched by the first light of the morning sun, a giant stone cliff atop a mountain imploded with an ear-splitting noise. The ancestors of the *Atayal* emerged from the stone cliff. They treated one another with love and respect and gradually learned from their natural environment how to live, and through their observations of animals, they even learned how to produce future generations of progeny.

Long, long time ago there were no humans on the earth. In the midst of what we now call Taiwan's Central Mountain Range, a huge stone cliff protruding into the open sky, would catch the first rays from the sun as it rose from the east.

Smooth, lustrous, and exquisitely formed, the precipice had been shaped by the passage of countless years, countless seasons, and countless cycles of greeting and bidding farewell to the sun and moon as they made their cycles. All through the years the stone face absorbed the essences of the elements.

One day as the dawn winds were rustling with a "swissshhing" sound, the first light from the east brushed upon the center of the stone cliff.

Suddenly, "CRACCCKKK!!!" came a thunderous sound as the cliff split in half. Three people, two men and a woman, came forth from the opening in the stone cliff. At first they were disoriented by this new and strange world before them. Soon however, their confusion gave way to curiosity. They wandered all about taking in their new and wonderful surroundings.

One of the men was terrified at the thought of how he would survive among the treacherous cliffs, perilous jungles and unfathomable lakes. The more he thought about it the more agitated he became. Finally, he turned around and lept back into the open crevice of the giant stone.

The others were following and were stunned to see him returning to the giant stone. Running after him they tried to dissuade him from going back, to persuade him to join them together in their new life.

But before they knew it, "HSSSIIAAH!!!", the crevice closed suddenly and the giant rock appeared as though nothing had happened. There was not a trace of the man who had returned into the cliff.

The other man and the woman quietly accepted their destiny of just the two of them to spend their lives together.

They lived mostly on the abundant wild vegetables and fruits of the mountains and forests. Sometimes the physically powerful and stalwart man would hunt deer and wild rabbit, or catch fish and shrimp from the mountain streams, while the clever and dexterous woman used her skills to make clothes from the animal hides.

When they were not working they liked to sit beneath the trees watching the sika deer frolicking in the forest meadows, and listening to the birds singing in the trees.

 **What's more?**

pinsebugan: this *Atayal* word literally means "to split open". This *Atayal* creation story is located in the mountainous area or *Masitoban* which is in Nantou County, Ren-ai County, Fasiang Village. According to the *Atayal* tradition, their first ancestors were born out of the splitting open of this giant stone.

Land of the treacherous cliffs, perilous jungles and fathomless lakes: the *Atayal* traditional habitat was largely in the area of high mountains of two to three thousand meters.

The earth was at peace. There was harmony in nature and they liked nothing more than to watch and learn from the animals, ever adding to their knowledge about how to live in the natural environment.

Time thus passed in the mountains and forests. Countless days of leisure and happiness. However, in watching the ways of the animals, they discovered these fellow inhabitants were able to procreate and carry on from generation to generation. This piqued their curiosity.

They were especially excited to see four or five little birds emerge from a nest.

So too were they fascinated when they observed how the deer frolicked in the meadows like spirits of the mountain. Sometimes they would observe a coquettish little deer running all about playing with its mother. The man and woman felt a slight tinge of sorrow.

Beneath a fallen tree they would watch groups of ants working in concert to carry great bits of food that one ant alone could never hope to move. They envied these congregations of families and friends, and often reflected on the fact that they were the only humans around. It was very lonely, just the two of them.

How to generate the next generation of their species? They were confused and really had no clue as to how they could create more people to keep them company.

In order to engender future generations of their species they tried everything. Could children be produced from their ears? From their mouths? Eyes? Noses?

Unfortunately, all their efforts to produce children were in vain.

The woman recalled that when she and the two men first emerged from the stone cliff, she had felt a light and pleasant wind sweeping over the giant stone.

Thinking that she may have solved the puzzle of procreation, the woman climbed up the mountain. She was surrounded by the beauty of stone cliff. Sitting on the edge of the cliff, she spread her legs wide apart and let the light breeze waft over her entire body. She hoped this would bring a child.

But still no child.

The more they tried and failed, the more distressed they became.

One day they were resting and watching flies buzzing and flying about. They suddenly noticed that two of the flies were not in the air but were lying on top of one another copulating on the ground.

The two suddenly realized that this was the way to procreate!

Having been inspired by the flies they had a silent understanding. If there was to be another generation of their species, the time had come for them to join together.

However, the man felt a little awkward at this because they seemed more like brother and sister than husband and wife. After all, they had both come out of the great rock and they had been living together for such a long time! He was too shy to make love with the woman.

For her part, the woman understood the man's thoughts but she also knew how important to humanity it was for them to bear children. Moreover, having seen the joy of the other animal mothers with their young, she longed for a child!

She resolved to come up with a plan to set the man at ease so they could have children.

One day the man awoke and discovered the woman was gone. This was the first time he had ever been alone! Frantically he searched everywhere. As if gone mad, he ran up and down mountains one by one in the hopes of finding her. However, when could find no trace of his companion he was both apprehensive and heartbroken.

Later on, just at twilight following a day of searching, he was dejectedly returning to his abode when suddenly, from behind a big tree next to a stream, the image of a person flashed before him.

His senses sharpened immediately and he ran in pursuit of the apparition. Finally catching up, he found it was a woman!

He was very happy and excited over this unexpected event. At first he thought that he had found the woman with whom he had lived for so long, however, this woman's face was dark and swarthy, a face he did not recognize.

Although he was disappointed at not having found his original mate, he did not want to spend his days alone, so he consoled himself at having found a new companion. They returned to the camp and that evening the two made love.

The next morning the man awoke from a deep sleep and the sweetest of dreams. He looked over and saw the strange woman washing her face. But when she turned around, he shouted out "WAAAAHHHH" in surprise. This woman was not a stranger, but his lost companion! The man was overjoyed to be together again, and very touched by how she had made such efforts bring them together.

The woman was smart enough to know that the bashful man would not dare make love to her, so she decided to leave him for a time and darken her face with ashes so that he would not recognize her. Thus disguised, she returned and they became lovers.

It was not long before the woman gave birth to their first child. The man and woman had completed their mission of procreation. These were the original ancestors of the *Atayal*.

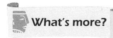 **What's more?**

Abodes of Atayal: Traditionally *Atayal* lived in bamboo houses with beams of keyaki and cypress wood. The sides and rooves generally used makino bamboo, or in places where there was no mikino, the sides would use split wood was used for the sides and slivers of cedar were used for the rooves.

matas: the *matas* is the customary face tattoo of the *Atayal*, a tradition passed down from this story when the woman disguises herself by darkening her cheeks.

02

The Magical Summons

In days long past the *Atayal* people's needs for the meat of the wild boar, fresh mountain spring water, wood for the fire, millet and all else to maintain a healthy and happy life could be instantly summoned. There was no need to work the fields, hunt, fetch water or chop wood. However, when our hearts and minds become tainted with greed and sloth, and when we betray nature's generous bestowal of her bounty, all people will succumb to a life of toil and strife..

There was a time, long long ago, when our *Atayal* ancestors did not have a care in the world.

We passed relaxed and happy days, nothing like the toil and struggle we face today by planting or hunting. We had all we needed to eat and wear we lacked nothing.

Anything and everything to sustain our lives came to us by simply calling out our needs.

For example, if we wanted to eat mountain boar, we needed only to shout out "*vha*", "*vha*", "*vha*", and a mountain boar came to us.

 **What's more?**

> **pqumah and mnayang:** these are two kinds of *Atayal* farming techniques. The former was done by women and was a very environmentally-friendly type of planting seed in shallow soil and clearing weeds by hand. The other, also known as "slash and burn" applied fire to burn the vegetation off an area of the mountain. The residual ash from the fire was a rich natural fertilizer.
>
> **bzyok qnhyun:** the mountain boar is called out by *Atayal* with the sound "*vha*".

Even more fantastic, we could pluck a few hairs from the boar, place them in a bamboo container and in a few moments, we would remove the container's cover and the hair would have become delicious boar meat, a grand feast.

We used this magical call to summon other wild animals, fish, shrimp, honey, fruit, anything we wanted.

When we needed fresh water to rinse the food, we needed only to call out "*qsya*", "*qsya*" and the water vessels would fill to the brim with mountain spring water.

We never needed to go to the mountains to hunt or go to the rivers to fish. We didn't need to exhaust ourselves with tasks such as going to fetch water from the river. Everything we needed was provided for. We simply shouted out the magical summons.

How about rice and other grains? No problem. Although we did some farming at the time, it was so much less effort than the farming done today.

All farming consisted of tending to one's family plot of rice or millet by daily watering. When ready for harvest, one bundle of grain could feed a family for an entire year.

And when cooking rice, we just placed one grain in the pot with no need to first rinse it. This one grain would become a big pot of delicious, fragrant hot steamed rice, enough for everyone to eat their fill.

When going on a long trip, we would tuck a few grains of rice in our *qengay* and have plenty to eat for many days.

How did we get firewood for cooking the rice?

Of course, by giving out the magical summons! Simply by shouting out "*qhunig*", "*qhunig*" we would have more than enough firewood piled up before own doors and windows. Upon being summoned the wood would pile itself up next to the stove, all ready for the fire.

 **What's more?**

> **yawa:** a cooking utensil made of bamboo in which things such as sweet potatoes and yams can be cooked.
> **qsya:** *Atayal* word for water.

Although they did not need to labor long hours or struggle to survive, our ancestors bore great respect and reverence for all things. Nothing was wasted, nothing taken for granted. And thus did our Atayal ancestors pass their days in a state of harmony and happiness.

But these days did not last.

One day as a woman was calling out "*vha*", "*vha*", "*vha*" to summon a mountain boar, she succumbed to feelings and thoughts of greed.

She thought to herself, "Hmmph, every time we take the hairs from the boar to prepare a meal, the amount of meat is just enough, it is not really filling. I bet if we cut the meat from the boar directly there would be even more!"

Just at that time a boar ran up to her. Without hesitation she whipped out a knife and sliced off the boar's ears.

The boar cried out "*ywak – ywak - ywak*" and scurried off deep into the mountains.

The boar told all the other animals about the cruelty of the greedy woman. An old deer king listened to the story and then said with tears in his eyes: "Ahhh, we animals showed pity for the human because of their need to toil and sweat to make a living. Who would have thought that our earnest efforts to meet their needs for food would meet with such cruelty? So be it! From now on there is no need to help the humans."

What's more?

Farming: for the *Atayal* farming consisted mainly of planting and harvesting crops. Their important crops were upland rice, millet, quinoa, yam, as well as pigeon peas, peanuts, ginger, greens, plantain, ramie, fuchsia and tobacco.

qengay: to enhance a person's attractiveness *Atayal* at around the age of seven or eight would have the ears pierced, with a plant stalks placed in the hole. Gradually more and more of the stalks were added until the hole could hold a piece of bamboo. This was generally done during the cold weather of winter.

qhunig: *Atayal* word for firewood.

ywak: the noise made by a mountain boar in pain.

Thereafter the animals no longer ever responded to the humans' calls. If the human wanted to eat meat they would have to go into the mountains and hunt, sometimes encountering vicious bears. Only after they fought for and won their food could they be said to have earned the meal.

If they could no longer get their meat so easily, they still had their fragrant rice!

However, one woman's laziness upset the rice. That woman thought: "Every time I prepare rice I can only make enough for one meal. What a lot of bother! If I could make enough to last for many days wouldn't that be much better? Couldn't I take more time to relax?"

Instead of just one grain, enough to feed the whole group, the lazy woman threw a big handful of rice into the *kluban*. When the rice was boiling *kluban* began rattling and shaking as though it were going to explode.

When the lazy woman removed the lid of the *kluban*, she shrieked in surprise as within a split second the grains of rice turned into a flock of *pzit*. With a cry of "bur! bur! bur!" they flew out of the pot.

The lazy woman was so shocked that she was unable to talk and could only watch as all the birds flew out of the house. She could hear the *pzit* chattering among themselves: "Lazy humans! Lazy humans! From now on, there will be no more carefree days for you! You will have to sweat in the fields planting, and tending to your crops if you want to harvest anything!"

She also heard the *pzit* laughing and talking among themselves. They were taunting the people: "Before you have a chance to reap that which you have spent so much

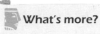

What's more?

kluban: this is the word for cooking pot. Before they had this implement *Atayal* used hollowed out Phoenix trees (*genus Firmiana*) for cooking vessels.

mnayang: much of the area inhabited by *Atayal* is steep mountain slope leading to their development of special techniques to use the land, including a slash and burn method of agriculture. After using such land for two or three years they planted alder trees (*Alnus formosana*) to let the land rest while they moved on to another area.

pzit: sparrow.

sweat and effort on, we will go into your fields and help ourselves, feasting on the rice and other grains! So work hard, and spend lots of effort to watch over your fields, lest all be eaten by us!"

The birds chattered on as they flew out the window and into the woods.

But the people's troubles were not over yet.

Another tragedy was caused by a young man. This young man simply didn't like to work and just wanted to play tricks on people all day. He often pestered young women and was disliked by everyone.

One day when he was walking in the mountain he came across a pile of firewood *"doong, doong, doong"* as it clattered its way to someone's home for their cooking fire.

The young man thought it would be fun to play a trick, so he hid in the grass along-side the mountain path and when the firewood passed by, he suddenly shouted out: "WAAAAAHHH". The firewood was so startled that it fled in all directions to hide in the forest. The firewood couldn't recover from the shock and didn't dare go near people again.

So from this day on, when people wanted fuel for cooking or heating they had to spend lots of time and energy to cut, gather, and haul their firewood.

Humans betrayed nature's goodwill. They responded to nature's bounty with abuse, greed and foolishness. There once was a time when the mountain boar, the wild deer, spring water, the wood of the forest, millet and other grains all believed in and had faith in humans. But after being taken for granted, or worse, after being abused or neglected, they would no longer offer up their bounty. To sustain our-selves we Atayal now have to work at planting, hunting, carrying water, chopping and collecting firewood.

That's why our Atayal elders urge their children and grandchildren to avoid waste, shun greed, and not to play harmful pranks. These attitudes are not only to be ad-opted in dealings with other people, but also in interaction with the animals, trees, grains, water and all of nature.

The Rainbow's Judgment

> Without exception, when a member of the *Atayal* tribe dies, his or her soul must pass over a rainbow bridge to the spirit world. This passage is the person's "judgment". Success in making the passage is only for those persons who lived their lives with courage and virtue, it is only for those who have acted appropriately and in accordance with gaga, the customs and principles of the tribe.

The beautiful rainbow that reveals itself in the clear sky following a rainstorm always evokes a sense of awe and delight.

But in the eyes of *Atayal*, the rainbow has a deeply spiritual significance. The elders of the tribe often admonish children: "It is taboo to point with your finger at the 'rainbow spirit bridge', you must never do this."

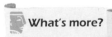 **What's more?**

hongu utux: this word for rainbow in *Atayal* also means the "spirit bridge". *Atayal* believe that after people die their spirits all go to the eternal realm of spirits to meet with the spirits of their ancestors. From the realm of human activity to the realm of the spirits one must embark on a slow and distant journey. At the entrance to this realm is an exquisite bow-shaped rainbow bridge over which all souls of the dead must pass.

psaniq: for *Atayal*, violation of social and community customs and conventions include those relating to daily life (for example relations between men and women, hunting taboos), ritual (for example prior to performing the ritual, contact with outsiders should be avoided), and must be carefully attended to so as not to anger the spirits who may otherwise visit disaster upon the individual or the tribe.

According to *Atayal* legends, the rainbow is the bridge to '*tuxan*, and it possesses the power to review all human affairs, to determine matters good and evil, of right and wrong.

The legends say that the rainbow spirit bridge was originally a human known as *Buta*. *Buta* went through a magical transformation to become the rainbow. Here is the story of how that happened.

Buta was a fearless man of boundless strength. He could fight the ferocious black bear using his bare hands. But *Buta* was not only a great hunter, he also understood and conducted his daily affairs in accordance with *gaga*. The Atayal's admiration for *Buta's* heroic feats was no greater than their respect for his character. *Buta* naturally became the role model and spiritual leader of the *Atayal*.

Buta's advice was sought whenever there was a problem within the tribe. He was

 **What's more?**

'**tuxan:** the realm of the spirits.

buta: the word buta subsequently was joined with the honorific prefix "gun" to become known as "*gun-buta*". *Atayal* firmly believe that *gun-buta's* soul transformed into the rainbow bridge at the edge of the spirit realm and all persons after death, no matter male, female, old or young, will receive the judgment by passing over the rainbow bridge.

gaga: is the general term *Atayal* use for all customs, conventions, rules to live by, as well as the cultural beliefs and practices followed by all tribal members. gaga carries a range of meanings, for example, it may signify the tribe's mutual aid, and at the same time, groups will have shared standards of right and wrong, good and evil and will jointly conduct ceremonies in connection with opening new land for crops, planting, harvest, building a house or other activities. This mutual support signified by *gaga* is an important element in the cohesion of the *Atayal* as a tribe and for each individual member.

mrhuw: this word in *Atayal* means spiritual leader. Among *Atayal* there is no aristocracy or class system. The spiritual leaders of the Atayal community are the elders, the brave, the wise and the fair and just. mrhuw is not passed down from father to son and is thus different from the chief or aristocracy systems in other tribes.

righteous and fair. He could deal with any dispute. Even the most stubborn of people would follow *Buta's* advice.

The members of the tribe sought *Buta's* counsel on all important matters: in matters of hunting, planting, harvests, and ceremonies.

Buta devoted all of his ability and energy to serving his people. The *Atayal* respected and revered him as though he were a god.

Just before *Buta* died, he spoke to the tribe: "After I die I will become a rainbow. I will be high overhead watching and protecting generations to come. But you must remember to uphold the gaga. The gaga is your ancestors' gift to you." No sooner had he finished speaking than he closed his eyes and passed from this world.

All of a sudden, a spectacular rainbow appeared in the sky above. This was the transformation of *Buta* into the rainbow bridge. The bridge traversed the world of the humans and the world of the spirits. The deeds of all Atayal would be reviewed and judged at their deaths by this rainbow. And all judgments would be in accordance with gaga passed down by the ancestors of the *Atayal*.

According to the ancient teachings of *Atayal*, men were expected to devote themselves to becoming brave hunters. They hunted mountain boar, deer, black bear, and other animals. Sometimes they hunted other humans to take their heads.

Women, according to the teachings, were supposed to be industrious and accomplished weavers and planters.

If a male had lived his life by the principles and teachings of the gaga, when he died, the souls of all the animals and people that he had killed would gather together and accompany his spirit in a grand march into the realm of the spirits.

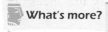

What's more?

mgaga: the m prefix before the word gaga in *Atayal* makes the noun a verb, that is to say, the modified word becomes something to be implemented. So if *gaga* is the *Atayal* general term for rules, law, ritual, mgaga means the execution of the ancestor's traditional mores. Thus in times past, the activity of hunting for the enemy's head was a sacred act.

Entering the world of the spirits with such a splendid procession would attract the attention of the spirits of the ancestors, and they too would come forward to meet the newly arrived. For a person who had lived by the *gaga*, facing these spirits was an event of pride and honor, there were no feelings of fear or regret.

On the other hand, some people had lived their lives in a cowardly, thoughtless and clumsy manner. They had been frivolous and lazy. For them, their fate was to enter the world of the sprits alone and isolated. No spirits of ancestors or other beings would be at the rainbow bridge to greet them.

As people approached the entrance to the spirit realm, *Buta*, manifest as the rainbow bridge, stood before them. Beneath the bridge was a deep ravine harboring ravenous poisonous snakes, giant pythons, and vicious crocodiles.

So while the brave and upright would boldly and confidently cross space the rainbow bridge, effortlessly entering the realm of the spirits, the cowardly and lazy faced what seemed to be an enormous and intimidating task. Rather than attempting to cross the bridge to the world of the spirits, many souls would try to find another way. However, any path other than crossing the rainbow bridge was so long and treacherous that those souls who attempted to avoid the rainbow's judgment, would lose their way, forever wandering, alone and unable to enter the realm of the spirits.

Many of those who had not lived by the *gaga* during their time in the human world, and who failed to reflect on their errant ways, might still insist on crossing the rainbow bridge. When they were half way across, the bridge would erupt in contortions and the lost soul would be thrown into the deep abyss, becoming food for the giant pythons and crocodiles.

For *Atayal*, the deafening sound of thunder accompanying a rainbow high overhead, is the voice of *Buta* reminding them: "Do not spend your days in obstinate, wasteful and frivolous activities: follow the ways passed down by the ancestors, live by the *gaga*".

布農族
B u n u n

01

Rendezvous with the Moon

> Two suns were too much for the world. Everything was dying from the intense heat. A father and his son decided to shoot one of the suns for the sake of their survival. After a great struggle they blinded one of the suns and it became the moon. They made a pact with the moon and from this came all of the customs, rituals and taboos of the Bunun. All *Bunun* remember the promise made to the moon and none dare renege on the words of their ancestors.

Long long ago during the great chaos, two suns in the sky took turns shining on the earth and so there was never any respite from the heat. With the temperature was always so hot plants and animals struggled to survive and could hardly reproduce future generations.

One family of *Bunun* worked in the fields every day despite the excruciating heat. They had no choice, for it was from the fields that they made their livelihood. When they went to the fields to work they set their infant by the side of the field and used the leaves of the giant taro plant (*bulaktai*) to shade him from the sun.

However, under this kind of heat the leaves quickly charred and became black.

The child's father tried to use banana leaves instead of the bulaktai but still they became charred and were no protection from the sun. Even stranger and more upsetting was that the child perished from the heat and turned into a lizard!

The infant's father was so upset by the tragedy of his child's death that he vowed to wage battle with the sun. On behalf of all his people he declared that he would shoot the sun out of the sky.

Thereupon, the father and his eldest son packed up their millet and other provisions before setting off on their mission to shoot the sun.

Not long after they had set out they stopped to plant the tree of *izuk*. Then they quickly went off toward the place of the sunrise. Day after day they searched for a good place from which they could shoot their arrows into the sun.

After walking for who knows how long, they came to a high plateau with a good view. They waited there for the moment of the sunrise. As the sun gradually began to appear and slowly ascended, they prepared their bows and arrows.

But the sun became stronger and stronger until it was just too much to bear. They could not even open their eyes, and were unable to get the sun into focus. Finally, using *asik* leaves to block out some of the brilliant sun, and with all the skill they could muster, they let their arrows fly. At last they succeeded in shooting and arrow into the sun's left eye.

 What's more?

The great chaos: among the *Bunun*, the great chaos is known as a very mysterious age where all sort of unimaginable things might happen.

vali: is the *Bunun* word for "sun" and in their culture the sun, unlike the moon, has no special significance.

isiun: is the word for lizard in the *Bunun* language.

izuk: is the *Bunun* word for sweet tangerine. The father and son planted the tree on their way to shoot down one of the suns, and by the time they returned it was already bearing fruit, signifying the long time they took in their quest to shoot down the sun. The *izuk* is a type of pomelo and in 1996 Du Shih-luan, the recorder of this story on a visit to the abandoned residence of taki hunang in Hsin-yi Township, Nantou County discovered such a sweet tangerine tree. Currently in three of Taiwan's northern counties -Taoyuan, Hsinchu and Miaoli – some farmers still cultivate this fruit and the Hakka people often use these tangerines in their offerings to ancestors.

They shot another arrow into the sun's left eye and gradually the intensity of its brilliance declined, and as it flickered and sparked in chaos, it transformed into the moon.

The sun's left eye had been blinded by their arrows!

Now, the entire earth began to change. Night and day became separated. What once was one of the suns was now the moon and she came out at night. The remaining sun came out in the day.

Since there was now only one sun, the climate became much more temperate. Night and day were now clearly distinct with temperature; varying significantly be between night and day. Soon the ecology of mountains, rivers, animals and plants all changed to adapt.

Having completed their mission the father and son happily returned to their village. But the sun they had shot with their arrow had other ideas and tried to stop them.

The father and his son ran for their lives. With all their effort they were able to jump through the spaces between the fingers of the sun, but eventually they were caught.

The sun (now the moon), using her fingers applied her spittle. Stuck together she flicked them into her palm. The father and son were so frightened that they were shaking all over when the sun/moon very calmly said to them:

What's more?

asik: is the *Bunun* word for a low-altitude shade-tolerant plant "mountain palm". Its red fruit is astringent and sweet, and its tender stems are delicious wild vegetables. In early days, Taiwanese often used them to make brooms and robes; and when Bunun go outdoors to work, they often put the braided leaves on their backs to protect them from the sun.

buan: is the *Bunun* word for the moon. With their animistic beliefs everything is a spirit, including the moon. The moon and the Bunun have a very close relationship. They regard the moon as a living spirt and use the cycles of the moon to calculate time in a manner similar to the lunar calendar we use today. The moon's phases - from the first quarter, to the full moon, to the last quarter, the stars around the moon, and even the halo surrounding the moon all have their particular significance and meanings.

"Why did you hurt me like this? I don't want to take revenge or kill you, but I do want you to make three promises. Then I will release you so that you may go tell your tribe that they must abide by these promises lest the entire tribe be destroyed."

"First, you must observe my comings and goings and all my changes. You must use all kinds of ritual to remember me. I will protect your millet harvest and other produce. You will have enough for your needs."

"Second, you must have taboos and prohibit all improper behavior in order to establish an orderly and just society."

"Third, throughout your people's lives they must always perform tribute to life and communicate respectfully with the spirits. This will affirm the value of people's lives in this world."

When the father and son acknowledged that they would comply they were set free.

Bearing their oath to the moon, the father and son traveled a great distance for several years before they finally arrived back in their village. They came to the izuk they had planted at the beginning of their quest and it had grown big and tall full of ripe, sweet and succulent tangerines.

They never forgot their promises to the moon, and upon arriving home the first thing they did was to call all their tribe together to make an announcement:

What's more?

Iusan: is the *Bunun* word for telling the propitious times for rituals according to the changes in the moon.

samu: is the *Bunun* word for taboo, the original being their pact with the moon which could not be violated, but later this was extended to taboos regarding daily life, foods, language, marriage between relatives and so on. However, even among the *Bunun* there are differences from tribe to tribe or village to village.

Ritual: ritual is an intimate and essential part of the *Bunun's* entire life: ritual for delivery from the womb, ritual for infancy, for *malagtainga*, for eradicating disease, marriage, death, etc.

"From now on we must strictly follow the commandments of the sun/moon whose left eye was shot by an arrow."

"She will come out every thirty days or so. When she appears we must pay tribute to her!"

"In the course of every person's life there is a system of customs and traditions. There must also be a set of taboos in order to regulate the way we behave in society. If we can comply with the promises made to the moon, the *Bunun* will enjoy eternal prosperity."

"And if we do not follow these customs our tribe will be destroyed."

From this time on the *Bunun* developed their customs and traditions. They frequently conducted ceremonies and rituals with many complex procedures. These are the origins of the rules, customs, rituals and taboos of the *Bunun* today.

Where did it come from?

This story was collected from the village of sal-itung in Hsinyi Townshiip, Nantou County.

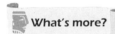 **What's more?**

lamungan: is the *Bunun's* original home located in today's Nantou County between Chushan and Mingjian. However, this place has no relation to the location of the father and son in this story.

Etiquette and ritual: The Bunun do not separate etiquette and seasonal rituals. The two are collectively referred to as "*lusan*" although anthropologists distinguish between the two in order to try to understand the *Bunun* culture. Life rituals include pregnancy, childbirth, choosing names, infancy, malaqtainga, coming of age, marriage, death, and so on; seasonal rituals repeated each year include those for cultivation, sowing, weeding, selection, repelling birds, harvesting, storage, and so on.

02

The Story of Adal

> Even though she had been kidnapped by the *Amis*, *Adal* never gave up or forgot her *Bunun* village. With extraordinary skill and courage, she finally found a way to take her child back to their home. Although *Adal* finally turned into a nightingale, her son *Diang* learned many things from her that would make him one of the most courageous and talented leaders of the *Bunun*. He learned to respect others and was able to establish a peaceful and prosperous *Bunun* village.

In times past *makavas* was an important part of the relations among the different tribes. For the *Bunun* it was also an important part in the social development of their young men.

The *Bunun* villages in what is now central Taiwan were often attacked from the east by the headhunting tribe who they called the *Bandalang* and who today are known as the *Amis*.

When one of the *Bandalang* head hunting groups was raiding a *Bunun* village

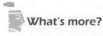

What's more?

Land of the rising sun: the *Bunun* lived in the western part of Taiwan's Central Mountain Range, hence the land of the rising sun is simply the areas east.

Bandalang: in the *Bunun* language *Bandalang* refers to the *Amis*.

makavas: headhunting was one type of warfare and was one was in which the Bunun males would gain social stature. It had been part of *Bunun* culture since time immemorial and was only gradually stopped during the Japanese era in Taiwan.

they discovered a beautiful *Bunun* woman named *Adal*. *Adal* was like the tender grains of spring millet, a young beauty of such graceful bearing that she captured the soul of everyone who saw her. The *Amis* kidnapped *Adal* and took her back to their own village.

Poor *Adal*! She had just married a man of the *Bunun* who was talented at playing the *qangqang*. She was also carrying his baby and now they were forced apart!

Adal wept all the way to the *Bandalang* village trying every means possible to escape her *Bandalang* captors. She nearly collapsed from exhaustion, but she always maintained her composure. It was her clear mind and will power that enabled her to break branches and leave signs along the trail. Someday when she escaped she would use these signs to find her way back.

After four days of thrashing through the forests they arrived at the *Bandalang* settlement of *Sabat*.

After the beautiful *Adal* arrived at *Sabat* she was forced to be the wife of the chief of the settlement and soon thereafter she gave birth.

The chief of the *Sabat* settlement called this child *Maiyau kumul* while they changed *Adal's* name to *Iuatan*.

But Adal secretly called her son *Diang*. *Diang* was a beautiful young baby boy. Everyone in the village knew that his father was of the *Bunun*, but no one told this to *Diang*.

As *Diang* grew up, just as all the other young men in *Sabat*, he had to learn and participate in all the ceremonies and rituals, take turns on the watchtower over-

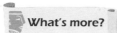

What's more?

Adal: the name *Adal* is seen in the *TanaPima* family which is part of the social systems of the Takbanuaz and *Takivatan* communitiies, located in the Tasi area of the Central Mountain Range.

qangqang: a bow shaped musical instrument plucked with the fingers while held in the mouth. The music produced has a soothing yet mysterious quality.

Sabat: this is the *Bunun* name for a village on Wuhe plateau in Ruisui Township, Hualian County. It is said that the stone pillars seen along the county road in Wuhe villiage were part of the home of the chief of the *Sabat* settlement.

looking the fish nets of the Siugulan River basin, and take his share of responsibility for other matters of their village.

However, *Diang*, being different from the other boys on account of his origins was subject to taunting, exclusion, humiliation and sometimes group bullying by the *Bandalang* village boys. They sometimes deprived him of food or even intentionally injured him hunting, claiming they had made a mistake.

Diang put up with this treatment for years. But one day when the head of the village was away *Diang* could not bear it any longer and he went to his mother and broke down crying, "Why are the spirits so unfair? I have followed all the rules of the village; I have not stolen anything or otherwise misbehaved. Why is it that every time I join in a village activity the others gang up on me and treat me so poorly? What have I done to deserve this fate? Does my face have some bad marks on it? Have I done something else wrong?"

Adal could only console him and tell him to continue to do things as the elders instruct. She dared not tell him anything about his true origins.

But *Adal* also told *Diang* that every time he was sent to the millet fields to work, he should take a small handful of millet grain and place it beneath the western mountain located next to the fields. She told him to be sure to keep the grain in a dry place.

Although *Diang* didn't understand what this was about, he did exactly as he was told by *Adal*. Every time he went into the fields he took a little bit of grain with him when he left, and stored it in the hills next to the mountain.

After a year he had stored up quite a large bag of millet.

One day when the village was celebrating haihai, and all the villagers were crowded together while the chief was busy serving in his role as *paliskadan lusan*.

What's more?

Diang: when giving a name, the *Bunun* generally follow principles of a kinship system so in this case *Diang* took the name of his paternal grandfather, *Adal's* husband's father.

Fish nets: *Amis* are known for their fishing skills, mostly using octagon nets, and sometimes basket traps and spearfishing.

mabazu: this is the *Bunun* word for millet that has been placed in a mortar and had its hull removed with a pestle.

Adal thought the time was right. She told *Diang* that when he returned from the fields that day, instead of coming back to the village, he should go to the western mountain where the grain was stored and wait for her.

Diang was puzzled by this, but he did as he was told and went to the place he had hidden the millet. Soon *Adal* arrived. She explained everything from the beginning, and now he finally understood the bullying and mistreatment.

"*Diang*," she told him, "we are not of this village. We are originally from the *Bunun* tribe. When I was pregnant with you the *Bandalang* head hunters of *Sabat* village attacked us and took me away to this place. You are *Bunun*! Today I am going to take you back to our home village – the days of mistreatment and bullying at the hands of the *Bandalang* are over!"

"*Bunun*!" exclaimed *Diang*, "at last I understand the wretched treatment I received."

Diang was determined to return with *Adal* to the embrace of their *Bunun* village.

They set off and as they traveled *Adal* carefully examined all the plants for the signs she left so many years ago. The branches she had broken or bent would now have grown in a way that was different than the other plants. Reading the signs in this way they went over many mountains and crossed many streams, traveling westward toward their *Bunun* village.

It was in the afternoon of the second day since they had departed *Sabat* when they first heard the sounds of the *Bandalang* warriors and their dogs. The barking of the dogs was growing louder and louder and it seemed as if they might catch up at any time.

The quick-witted *Adal* grabbed *Diang* and rushed to a nearby waterfall where they hid in a cave behind the curtain of the falls. The dogs were unable to pick up their scent and the *Bandalang* lost the trail. *Adal* and *Diang* were safe!

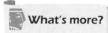 **What's more?**

hahais: this is the *Bunun* word for the *Amis* harvest festival.

paliskadan lusan: this is also a *Bunun* term for a person of the village who specializes in performing ritual other than those rituals related to warfare, similar to the *Amis* who would handle all the affairs of the village including the chiefs in charge of ritual and warfare.

Having left the soldiers and dogs behind, *Adal* and *Diang* continued their journey. Although they were exhausted, they continued to travel night and day. After several days their village was in sight.

It was late in the evening when they arrived and everything was very quiet. Adal relied on the light of the moon to find her old village that she had been missing for so long.

They arrived in the village and *Adal* held *Diang*'s hand as she searched for her family's home. Nearby they heard the familiar sound of a musical instrument. As they got closer *Adal* saw her husband playing the instrument and singing a song in remembrance of her.

With tears in her eyes and holding onto *Diang*'s hand, *Adal* quickly ran toward the music. But when she saw her husband, she discovered that he was not alone. There was another woman at his side. He had remarried!

Suddenly *Diang* noticed that the hand he was holding was cold. He turned to look at his mother but she was gone. All he could hear was the distant call of a nightingale singing her tragic song, "*salbu isang, salbu isang……*"

It was then that *Diang* realized that his mother had become a nightingale.

He was so upset that he knelt down and cried out "*tina, tina*" (mother, mother), but Adal would not return.

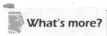

What's more?

pisdadaidaz: poem songs of sorrow, regret, mourning are sung by *Bunun* to express the suffering of losing a son, pining for absent relatives or ones misfortunes of fate.

Loss of one's wife: Although *Adal's* husband loved her, when the tribe members determined that she had been killed by the *Amis*, they forced him to marry another woman (all *Bunun* weddings at the time were arranged). He did not care for this woman, and spent his time playing music and pining away for his beloved *Adal*.

salbu isang: *salbu* is a *Bunun* word for sorrow and the phrase *salbu isang* means distraught and overcome with grief. *salbu isang* is also *Bunun* for "nightingale" named after the voice of the bird.

tina: this is the *Bunun* word for mother.

The years went by as *Diang* grew up in the *Bunun* village. On account of his rich experience and background, his strict adherence to the village rules and his diligence and respect for the elders, he was revered and respected and was soon recommended to be the lavian of the clan.

One hot summer day *Diang* was engaged in manipulating a divination *pistasiy*. On account of a propitious omen during the activity, he organized a group of *Bunun* headhunters to go to the east and find the *Bandalang* village of *Sabat*.

They came to the village of Sabat on the last day of the harvest festival when the Bandalang were completely off guard. Effortlessly the Bunun headhunters made their way to the great stone platform where the chief was resting. In the light of the summer moon, Diang attacked the chief and cut off his head. Traveling through the night, the Bunun warriors returned to their village.

Diang's villagers were ecstatic upon hearing the news *Diang's* actions had redressed the humiliation and erased the shame that the Bunun had borne for so long.

Diang's special background provided him with a keen ability to interact with others. He understood respect and cherished the opportunity to participate in the ceremonies of the tribe as well as the activities of the clan, the household and the village.

When he was of middle age *Diang* was made the "lavian" of the entire village. Under his leadership the village enjoyed peace and was free from strife and arguments. Their village won the praise and admiration for many generations to come.

Where did it come from?

This story was collected in the village of Kunuan, Wanrong township, Hualian County.

 **What's more?**

lavian: the *Bunun* word for leader of the warriors

pistasiy: the *Bunun* divination methods differ depending on the objective and who is conducting the divination. Ceremonial divination is done by the priest, and the head hunting divination is carried out by the military leader. First is the bird divination, dreams of that night are considered as are the various phenomena observed during the proceedings.

The Angry Hundred Pace Snake

> Qabus borrowed a baby snake from the mother Hundred Pace Snake to use while making clothes for her husband. But the baby died and the *Bunun* suffered the wrath of the Hundred Pace Snakes for many years. Then the *Bunun* led their own reprisals against the snakes. Fortunately, the two sides finally and wisely resolved their differences, became friends and lived together in peace.

Long ago in one of the *Bunun* villages there lived a husband and wife who were deeply in love with each other. The wife's name was *Qabus* and the husband's name was *Pima*.

Qabus usually took care of the household, the children, and the meals. She gathered plants around their home and she wove their clothes. All matters of the household, large and small, were handled by *Qabus*. *Pima* took care of the "outside matters" and the projects, such as hunting, headhunting warfare against the other tribes, planting the fields, and participating in the village festivals and rituals.

Qabus wanted to weave a beautiful suit of clothes for *Pima* to wear when he attended the ceremonies or took care of other village affairs. She wanted the clothes to be so wonderful that all the people of their village would admire them. This would bring honor to both her and her husband.

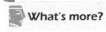

What's more?

outside matters: refers to matters such as village ceremony and rituals, participation in village water works and so on.

What sort of colors would be the most special? *Qabus* thought long and hard, comparing all the different animals for the best design. Finally she decided that the colors and patterns of the Hundred Pace Snake were the most beautiful. She made up her mind to weave *Pima's* clothes using colors and patterns from the Hundred Pace Snake.

One day *Qabus* came across a mother Hundred Pace Snake.

Gathering up all her courage, *Qabus* spoke to the snake and told her that she would like to borrow one of her children to use as a model for making the clothes.

At first the mother snake did not agree. After much begging and pleading by *Qabus* however, she finally gave in.

Although the mother snake agreed that *Qabus* could take one of her children back to the village to use as a pattern for her weaving, *Qabus* had to bring the child back to the mother snake within seven days.

After a few days *Qabus* completed the clothes. When her neighbors saw such beautiful patterns, they too wanted to use the Hundred Pace Snake's patterns, so they borrowed the baby snake from *Qabus*. Her neighbors then also wove beautiful clothing for their men.

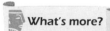

What's more?

Hundred Pace Snake: In *Bunun* there are two words for this animal: *kaviaz* which means friend, and *gavit* which means warning. *Bunun* take this animal to be their friend and not to be killed. When seen, one should tear off a piece of clothing and give it to the snake and say "you run along now, quickly!" When *Bunun* tear off a piece of clothing it indicates friendship, and is also a gift.

Men's clothing: clothes of male and female in the *Bunun* are quite different. Male clothing has no pants and is replaced by a T cloth to facilitate agile movement in hunting and warfare; for the upper body a vest is worn with pockets around the chest area to hold small items such as tobacco, pipes, and dried meat. Women wear short jackets with long sleeves embroidered along the edges, and for the lower body a half circle apron-like skirt reaching to the calves. Women's clothing includes a headdress and gaiters.

When the news of the beautiful clothes circulated throughout the village all the women wanted to borrow the baby snake. With everyone dying for use of the snake, they accidentally killed it.

The seventh day arrived and the mother Hundred Pace Snake came to *Qabus'* home to ask for her child back. *Qabus*, of course, could not keep her promise because the child was dead. But instead of telling the truth she said to the mother snake:

"I can't give your child back today. Please come back tomorrow!"

The next day the mother snake came back to *Qabus'* home as agreed. But *Qabus* gave her the excuse that she had lent the baby snake to someone else and could not return it that day.

The mother snake finally realized what had happened and was very upset. Fuming with anger, she said:

"You of the *Bunun* have killed my child and broken your promises. You had better be careful!" She then left *Qabus'* home.

One night during a typhoon while the rain was pouring and the wind was gusting through the village, all the *Bunun* villagers were sound asleep and didn't notice anything odd.

During the storm several large packs of Hundred Pace Snakes silently made their way into the village.

The snakes went into the homes of all the *Bunun* and bit every person they could find. They filled the people with the poisonous venom they had been storing up all winter and most of the people who were sleeping died from the poison.

The snakes then went out to the fields, the trails, the hunting grounds and anywhere else that they might come across people. Whenever a group of people were out together, without hesitation the snakes would attack. This plague of attacks by the Hundred Pace Snake wiped out more than half of the *Bunun*.

The *Bunun* were so upset at this slaughter that they mobilized all their people and vowed to take revenge. They would kill all Hundred Pace Snakes wherever they were found and litter the area with the dead bodies.

After many generations of feuding between the *Bunun* and the Hundred Pace Snakes, the two sides gradually began to rethink their positions. If they continued to feud it would go on forever, so they decided to try and make peace.

After discussing the matter they jointly decided the Hundred Pace Snake would give their pattern to the *Bunun* as the design for the *Bunun's* formal dress and the snakes would no longer attack the *Bunun*. The *Bunun* agreed that they would no longer slaughter the Hundred Pace Snake and would treat the snake with honor, respect and reverence.

Since the time of this agreement the Bunun and the Hundred Pace Snake have peacefully coexisted.

The *Bunun* now have two ways to refer to the Hundred Pace Snake. One is *gavit* which means "be warned", and the other is *kaviaz* which means "friend".

Even today the patterns, colors and designs of traditional *Bunun* clothing are based on the colors and designs of the Hundred Pace Snake.

Where did it come from?
This story was collected in the village of Iai dazuan, Hsinyi township, Nantou County.

The Hunter's Faith

> The hunters who would not admit defeat nor give the appropriate reverence to nature met with a tragic end. From this story we see that people should respect nature in order to avoid her reprisal; we see that using nature to fulfill their arrogant desires and taking unnecessary risks may lead to death. We must always remember to defer to nature and the power of the earth. The only way to true human prosperity is for people to make peace with and live in harmony with nature.

Once there was a *Bunun* village called *Maiasang*. Every year between the harvest and planting was the time for hunting. All of the youth in the village would go to their hunting grounds to hunt animals and gather useful plants.

This is the story about a group of hunters from one of the *Bunun* clans. They prepared for the hunt in their usual manner and after performing the customary rites, they set off with their hunting dogs. This time was a bit unusual as one of the hunters brought along his young child.

When they arrived at their hut they began hunting and tracking the wild deer. Every day they would bring their game back to the hut.

After several days the weather changed. It looked as though a strong typhoon was approaching. After lively discussion and debate the decided they would stop the hunt and return to their village as quickly as possible.

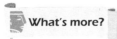 **What's more?**

The hunting season: generally occurs during the ninth and tenth months of the year and this is also the time for training young men in warfare so for the *Bunun* this is the time to learn martial skills, hunting, and archery.

During the discussion, the hunter who had brought his child suggested that they should not take any chances. He proposed that they wait for the storm to pass before making any decision. Whatever the others would do, he said he and his child would wait out the storm at the hut.

Most of the others thought this would be cowardly. Nearly everyone joined in saying "This storm is nothing! We have all been through storms before. What is there to worry about?"

Everyone then started packing up in preparation for their trip back to their village. They took all the provisions and the game they had caught, and extinguished the fire in the hut, leaving the man and his child to fend for themselves.

When the hunters were all gone, the man and his child quickly went over to the *banin* (fire pit) to restart the fire. They discovered a few burning embers so they quickly put on some dry tinder and feverishly blew on the coals. The fire was revived and they had a warm fire throughout the night of the typhoon.

The next morning the wind and rain had died down. Near their hut the child discovered a deer that had been killed by a falling rock. They cooked the deer over the fire and had a delicious meal. Soon the sun came out and the floodwaters receded. The man and his child packed up the remaining deer meat and made their way back along the hunter's trail to their village.

On the way back they made a horrible discovery. The supposedly brave men who went back to the village in the storm were all dead. Their bodies were mangled and some had limbs strewn here and there. It was obvious that the typhoon was a terrible one indeed.

As a memorial to the dead hunters the man and his son named each place where they found the parts of the bodies after that part of the body. This would be a reminder to people in the future of the infinite power of nature and that people should not believe that "man can conquer nature" as an excuse to destroy the environment, otherwise, as with the arrogant hunters, you may end up dead!

Where did it come from?

This story was collected in the village of sal-itung, Hsinyi township, Nantou County.

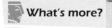 **What's more?**

banin: the word banin in *Bunun* means the place where food is cooked.

qailivan: is the *Bununs'* word for dried meat.

01

The Broken Arrow and the Two Tribes of the Tsou

Those of the *Tsou* Tribe fortunate to survive the great flood decided to split into two groups: *Tsou* and *Maya*. Each group would search for a place to settle. Upon the tearful departure they broke an arrow in half, each side vowing to keep their half for the day when they would be reunited.

Much later, when *Tsou* elders first encountered the Japanese, they believed them to be the lost tribe of the *Maya*, given their similar appearance. Where have the *Maya* gone? Alas, we still await the appearance of the other half of the broken arrow.

Long ago a huge eel lived at the lower reaches of the river. The eel was so big that when it laid itself across the river it was like a dam, and the water level was getting higher and higher.

The giant eel just would not move. Having nowhere to go, the water continued to rise until *Patungkuonu* was completely inundated.

The people that lived nearby had no choice but to move to higher ground. But the water kept rising. Finally, the only place that wasn't covered in water was the highest peak of *Patungkuonu*.

One day a giant crab discovered the eel. As the eel wasn't moving at all the crab thought it must be dead. With its pincer the crab grabbed the eel by its navel. Yeoucch! In great pain, the injured eel wildly thrashed its entire body and huge tail.

As soon as the giant eel moved all the water that had built up behind it began flowing into the sea. The vast expanse of flood waters finally receded; once again the people could see the mountains.

The *Tsou* people that were lucky enough to survive the great flood, came to appreciate even more the sanctity of all life, their fellowship with other people and the precious experience in having overcome adversity together. Those people who had taken refuge on Jade Mountain and who shared a common appearance and characteristics such as dress, customs, and language gathered in two settlements.

One group was known as *Tsou* and they settled in an area of Alishan known as *Tfuya*. The other group, known as *Maya*, went much further to the north and settled north of Taiwan in what is now Japan.

Upon taking leave of one another, the two groups broke an arrow in half, one half for the *Tsou* who went to *Tfuya* and the other half for the *Maya* who went to Japan.

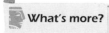

What's more?

Patungkuonu: a group of mountains referring to the Yushan Range. This *Tsou* name, *Patungkuonu*, is the name that became "*Batongguan*" well known in Taiwan by trekkers as one of the ancient trails on Yushan or Jade Mountain. This area is considered by the *Tsou* to be the sacred dwelling of the gods; the place where the gods created the *Tsou* people.

The two pieces of arrow would enable them to recognize one another in the future.

At the time most of the people went with the *Maya* group to Japan. But there are now very few of these people left... although even today, no one knows why this is.

Today the *Tsou* people still call the Japanese "*Maya*" being the only tribe of indigenous people to use this term for the Japanese. Perhaps this is their way of remembering the lost people of their tribe that hold the other half of the arrow.

Today *Tsou* elders still recall when the Japanese first came to Taiwan. They believed them to be the *Maya* returning after many generations. In part this was because the Japanese' appearance was similar to the *Tsou* people. Soon however they found their language, dress and customs were quite different. Nor did, the Japanese posses the other half of the arrow to prove the relationship.

The "*Maya*" remains a puzzle even today. No traces of these people have been found anywhere.

Where did it come from?

This story was collected from Chen Chuang-cih and Shih Ying-hsiung, two *Tsou* elders who were about eighty years old at the time of the interview. They are from the village of Pnguu, Chiayi County, Alishan Township.

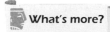 **What's more?**

Tfuya: this is one of the main settlements of the *Tsou* and is located in the area around Dabang village, Chiayi County, Alishan Township. In addition to Tapan, the main settlements of the *Tsou* include *Iuhtu*, *Hla'alua* and *kanakanavu*.

Facial features of the Tsou: *Tsou* people are of medium build, with straight noses and lustrous black eyebrows.

02

Revenge of the Mountain Boar

> The leader of the mountain boar took a liking to a beautiful woman. In the evening he transformed himself into a handsome man to meet with her. But the woman's brother brought an end to their relationship by taking the boar's life. The loss of their leader led to a frantic and frenzied retaliation by the mountain boar against the Tsou.
>
> The village was nearly wiped out. But a young man who had been out hunting during the attack, then brought on his own slaughter of the mountain boar thereby consoling his fellow tribespeople. From this time on the number of mountain boar dramatically decreased.

The *Tsou* people tell a story about a mountain boar that turned himself into a very handsome young man. He met a young and beautiful unmarried *Tsou* woman.

After he met the young woman, the mountain boar would spend all his time during the day living as a boar in the mountains and forests surrounding the *Tsou* settlement of *takupuyanou*. He followed the woman about all the time. He couldn't bear to be away from her for a minute.

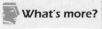
What's more?

takupuyanou: the settlement referred to in this story is *takupuyanou*. The settlement has disappeared and so far no records have been discovered.

In the evenings the mountain boar turned into a handsome man. He would then use all kinds of words and excuses to spend time and chat with the young woman.

The boar's initiative gradually became very attractive to the woman and the couple's relationship developed. The love struck boar would go into the woman's home and even spend the night with her.

They went on like this for some time and the young woman never discovered that her lover was in fact a mountain boar.

But one day, the young woman wondered to herself: "Why do I only see him at night? Why is he always gone with the first light of the morning?"

One evening the young woman's brother was returning home from a long day of hunting. He had not been at all successful in this instance and was quite dispirited. As he reached the entrance to *takupuyanou*, he suddenly saw a mountain boar pacing back and forth. His energy came back to him as he closely followed the mountain boar and prepared to make the kill.

When the mountain boar reached the young woman's home, he stopped. Just as the brother was about to shoot the boar with his arrow he saw something shocking!

Within a few short moments the mountain boar transformed into a person and nonchalantly entered the young woman's home. The brother was confused by this and waited by the door for his sister's lover to come out.

As expected, when the young man came out of his lover's home he turned back into a mountain boar,whereupon brother killed him using a long, sharp spear.

Hearing the screams of the mountain boar the young woman ran out to find that her lover was really a mountain boar. All the sweetness of their love suddenly became tragedy.

The mountain boar that had been killed was the leader of all the mountain boar in the area.

When the mountain boar's leader did not return the others knew that he had been hunted and killed by people. They then began to plan a vicious revenge for his death.

Tens of thousands of mountain boars from the entire area around *takupuyanou* converged to attack. Their ferocity terrified all in the village.

The strange sounds of the mountain boar emanating from the forests were signals to the people that they were about to be attacked.

Villagers gathered in the *Kuba* to discuss how to defend against the mountain boar.

It wasn't long before the settlement was in pandemonium. Once again the mountain boars were on the attack.

Fortunately the *Kuba* was high above the ground and the mountain boar were unable to climb up. They could only run about below, shrieking and snarling. From the *Kuba* the *Maotano* shot and killed many boars with their arrows.

But by the time the arrows of the *Maotano* were used up, the mountain boar were still viciously running about below. Efforts of the mountain boar to approach were thwarted by the sharp spears of the *Maotano*. Although the *Maotano* were exhausted, they continued to fight on to protect their people and their village.

After a while, so many dead mountain boar were piling up almost reaching the *Kuba*. It was getting very dangerous.

Before they knew it, the men inside the *Kuba* were facing the mountain boar that had climbed up on the dead bodies. The boars entered the *Kuba*, their sharp tusks slashing and killing all life inside.

Only after all the *Maotano* were dead, did the mountain boar finally begin to leave.

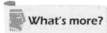 **What's more?**

Kuba: built from materials readily available to the residents such as wood and yellow rattan woven together with several layers of thatch for the roof, the *Kuba* stands about one and a half meters above the ground. The *Kuba* is used for many functions including the performance of ceremonies, training, and meetings. Only men are allowed into the *Kuba*. Meetings are generally attended by the heads of the different clans.

Maotano: to attain the status of *Maotano*, or warrior, one must have fought with a mature mountain boar, i.e., one that has already grown tusks.

During the attack of the mountain boar, far from *takupuyanou* in the mountains of *yamasiana*, one group of villagers were out hunting. On their return, they were merrily approaching *takupuyanou* eager to share their bounty with the villagers. But as they approached, they discovered that things were far from normal. Usually a crowd would come out to greet them. No one was around and things were unusually quiet. They had an eerie feeling that something must be wrong.

Returning to the *Kuba* they found corpses everywhere piled high. Struck with grief by the loss of their comrades, they pledged vengeance to the death.

While still recovering from the shock, they somehow managed to rationally assess the situation. They discovered that their people had been decimated by a gigantic butchering perpetrated by the mountain boar.

Furious, they vowed to take revenge against the mountain boar by no less than total extermination.

They set out at once, pursuing the footprints of mountain boar high and low, morning through night.

When they caught up with the mountain boar, there were so very many that a new strategy was necessary. They couldn't split up into groups lest they weaken their position. They finally decided to use their *phomeo*, the fires that they normally used during the hunt, to surround and exterminate the mountain boar.

Before the hunters had taken action, the mountain boar began mass movements. In hot pursuit the hunters calculated that the mountain boar would likely gather on the plains of ʻ*akuingana*. One group rushed ahead to prepare the *popsusa*, the fuel for their *phomeo*.

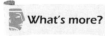

What's more?

yamasiana: this is the name of an area in the watershed of the Namasian Rivier located around the border of present day Kaohsiung.

phomeo: this is a hunting technique whereby fires are started upwind from the prey while the hunters and their hounds wait below to capture and kill their quarry.

They caught up with the mountain boar at '*akuingana* just according to plan. Taking advantage of the clamour and confusion among the mountain boar, fires were set to the surrounding dry plains. The flames spread rapidly. All routes to escape were cut off. Ceaseless, piercing screams of the mountain boar engulfed in a sea of flames continued until every last one was burned to death.

The plains became one great charred area but the smoke wafted far away to the villages as a kind of consolation for the souls of the people who had been massacred by the mountain boar. Peace finally returned to the mountains and forests.

It is said that this is when there began an obvious decline in the number of mountain boar in the area.

Where did it come from?
This story was created by the author based on narratives collected from *Tsou* elders.

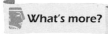 **What's more?**

'**akuingana:** in the *Tsou* language this means "the home of the firefly" and is located in present day, Laiji Village (Pnguu), Chiayi County, Ali Township.
Popsusa: the *Tsou* word for dry wood shavings.

The Forgotten Rites

> The ceremonies of *homeyaya* and *siuski* are the important fes-
> tivals for the *Tsou*. The "*homeyaya*" is when the people of the
> "small settlements" visit the people of the "large settlements"
> and "*siuski*" is just the reverse. These festivals bring the people
> of the *Tsou* together and serve as one way of maintaining their
> traditions and gratitude.

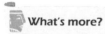 **What's more?**

Da She: this is the mandarin pronunciation for "large community". The word
"*she*" or community implies the inclusion of a *kuba* and hunting grounds,
and also in place where all kinds of ceremonies are performed. Examples
are *Tfuya* and *Taban*.

lilaci: this is the *Tsou* pronouciation for the village of Laiji in present day Ali
Township, Chiayi County.

soseongana: the place known to Taiwanese and many tourists as Ali Shan
or Ali Mountain is called *soseongana* by the *Tsou* and means the place
where there are a lot of pine or cedar trees. However during the Japanese
era many of these trees were cut down and the area was used for other
purposes including tree farms or artificial forests. We hope everyone can
help preserve the few remaining original forests in Taiwan.

The Large Settlement and the Small Settlement

The village of *Pnguu* is located on the northern part of Ali Shan Township in Chia Yi County. On the east is *hohcubu*, a sacred mountain. From *Pnguu* one looks in awe at *hohcubu* as it rises majestically and mystically into the sky. *hohcubu*, the eternal guardian of the *Tsou*, protects their lives and ensures the perpetuation of the tribe.

Lalaci was a special gathering place for the hunters from the large settlement "*Tfuya*". It has been around for at least two hundred years.

Why are there "large settlements" and "small settlements"?

Traditionally, the *Tsou* depended on hunting for their sustenance. When they first went out from the "large settlement", if they found game easily then they would return to the large settlement on the same day. But they often had to follow the game, and this might take them much farther away. As the area of their hunting grounds expanded, it became more common to not return to the large settlement on the same day. Thus, they built hnou or simple huts to stay in when they had to be away overnight.

Eager to spend more time with family members, the hunters began to bring their families to live in the outlying hnou.

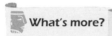

What's more?

Hunting: hunting is considered a serious and sacred undertaking by the *Tsou*. Prior to the hunt one must engage in "dream divination", give offerings to the mountain spirits in exchange for protection, safety and success during the hunt.

hupa: Hunting grounds were the living space or territory for each clan. The hupa was also an expression of the clan's consolidation of solidarity. It was forbidden for others to arbitrarily enter or exploit any but their own clan's hupa.

hnou: the materials used in the building of the *hnou* or hunter's lodge depended on what was handily available in the particular locale.

When the conditions of a particular location were favorable, the hunter would move the family. Gradually the number of families grew and soon there were a number of new "small settlements".

The hunters who lived in the small settlements still would pay homage to the large settlement. Every year at a specified time they would return to the large settlement. The *mayasyi* ensured interaction and continuity between the large and small settlements.

For example the village of *Pnguu (Lalaci)* was originally comprised of five families. Now it has grown to twelve.

In the past, the large settlement was the center of the social organization for the *Tsou*. All the important affairs, ceremony and rituals were handled or conducted at the large settlement.

Since the people in the village of *Lalaci* originated from the large settlement of *Tfuye*, the customs and rites of *Tfuye* are most important for the people of Lalaci. At all the festivals or other important occasions at *Tfuye*, all the families of *Lalaci* will return to participate in all the activities relevant to their clan.

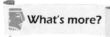 **What's more?**

> **mayasyi:** when the time comes to perform certain rituals such as the homeyaya or the mayasyi (the *Tsou's* traditional war ritual thanking the gods for protection in the past and asking for future success), the large settlement is the venue of choice, so the entire family living in the small settlement returns to the large settlement.

The *homeyaya* Festival

Many of the rites of the large settlement have been preserved down to this day. However, because of changes in the organization, many of the rites of the small settlements have been lost. The *siuski* is one of the rites that has been all but forgotten on account of the changes for the *Tsou* over the years.

What is the *siuski*? In order to understand this very old tradition, we first need to know about the *homeyaya* festival.

Every year when the people of the small settlement return to the large settlements to get together with family, they give a detailed report about what has been happening during the year in the small settlement. And if their hunting has been very successful, they will bring some of the game back to share with their relatives in the large settlement.

When they return to the large settlement it is very much like the atmosphere of the Chinese when they celebrate the Lunar New Year. The *Tsou* call this family celebration *homeyaya*.

So as *homeyaya* draws near, all the families of the small settlements or villages go to the large settlements to spend time with their families. There are no fixed "rules" as to how much time they can spend at the large settlements.

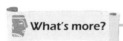

What's more?

Changes in the Traditional *Tsou* Social Organisation: The large and small settlements or communities of the were largely dismantled during the Japanese era through the forced relocation or creation of new administrative districts. Concurrent with this disruption, many of the traditional rituals and ceremonies also disappeared. The influx and influence of Han culture during recent years has exacerbated this loss.

siuski: the meaning of this word is "reciprocate" or "give back". The main function of the *siuski* was to bind the community, strengthen emotional ties and build consensus. It was the material that held *Tsou* society together and was vital in helping to preserve traditional *Tsou* culture. Through tremendous efforts of many people the siuski was revived on 5 May 2001 for the first time in 60 years in pnguu village, Ali Township, Chiayi County.

homeyaya: during the seventh or eighth month of the year when the millet is ready for harvest the *Tsou* celebrate homeyaya which is also known as the "millet harvest ceremony". The *Tso u* pay homage to the millet spirit at this time.

The *siuski* Festival

siuski is *homeyaya* in reverse. It is the time when the people from the large settlements go out to the small settlements to visit their relatives.

As the *siuski* approaches, residents of the small settlements get busy clearing the weeds along the roads leading to their settlement to demonstrate their welcoming of relatives. Also each clan will prepare their own fermented wine for their guests.

In the early morning of the *siuski* the calm is broken by the elders of the small settlement when they cry out in clear strong voices indicating the beginning of the festivities.

Everyone is busily moving about, visiting here, receiving visitors there. The spirit of celebration is everywhere.

Soon the smoke from the cooking fires is all over the place and the piercing sound of a mountain boar rings out. Although the sound almost hurts the ears, it signals that a feast of delicious food and fragrant wine is about to begin.

Around ten in the morning the guests from the large settlement begin arriving. Residents all dressed up in their brilliant red festive clothing gather in the plaza to greet the visitors. The ceremonies are about to begin.

About this time, when the chief of the large settlement, the elders, and all the male representatives of each family have arrived, they all walk to the entrance place that is about one kilometer from the village.

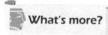

What's more?

around ten in the morning: In the past the *Tsou* kept time using the sun. Our twenty-four hour day was separated into four time frames of 3, 6, 9 and 12, but there were no names for a particular time segment. Rather, natural phenomena or the position of the sun would be used as a descriptor. So for example, 3 in the morning would be called "morning dew", 6 am "morning", 9 am "the sun before noon", 12 noon was simply "noon", 3 pm "the sun is preparing to set", 6 pm "dark sky" and so on.

Bright red traditional clothing: the *Tsou* do not attach any particular significance to different colors, however generally speaking, the color red is considered auspicious.

When they arrive at this entrance place they plant a sacred red banyan tree. This is the symbol of the *Tsou* Tribe. They also place here an image of *Pa'momutu*, guardian of the entrance to the village. The sacred red banyan tree is important because the spirits will attach themselves to this tree.

Once the red banyan tree has been planted and the Pa'momutu is in place, the settlement or village has been formally established and the *siuski* celebrations can proceed.

With all in order, the leader gives the command and all the people from the different villages or settlements hold hands forming a ring around the sacred tree. They sing the *ehoi* to welcome the spirits. With the conclusion of the singing phase, everyone returns to the village to continue with the other activities.

Following this is the time for the families to get together. The families of the small settlement invite the visitors from the large settlement so that the young people can become acquainted with each other. But for those who follow tradition, members of the same clan cannot marry.

The *Tsou* people with the Chinese names of An, Cheng, Wu and Yang do not intermarry because according to *Tsou* kinship system tradition people with these four names all come from the *yaisungu* clan.

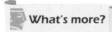

What's more?

yono: according to *Tsou* tradition when the spirits shook the red banyan tree, each of the falling leaves became a human, a member of the *Tsou* tribe. The tree, known as the tree of life, is considered sacred by the *Tsou*.

Pa'momutu: at the main entrance of settlements, the *Tsou* have a simple yet solemn ritual calling on the heavenly spirits to protect the tribe and can be compared to the Han people's reverence for the Tudi Gong or the land god. It is also a bit like an inspection station one sees at the entrance to military camps.

ehoi: this word literally means the "beginning of the song" and was sung using ancient *Tsou* language which *Tsou* can sigh but for they need to rely on elders for explanation.

Also, the elders use this family gathering to pass on to the younger generation the history of the tribe and all the events that led to the establishment of their settlement.

The *siuski* festival places great importance on the interaction between the large and small settlements and has always been one of the most important traditional activities of the *Tsou* Tribe. However, time passes and things change, so the festival has been neglected, even gradually forgotten by the *Tsou*.

Where did it come from?

This story is based on the author's interviews with elders during his participation in meetings of the 2001 Pnguu Community Development Association's siuski Festival Ceremony Preparatory Committee.

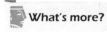 **What's more?**

yasiungu: A form of social organisation larger than a household but smaller than a small settlement. The *yasiungu* members share hunting grounds, fish ponds and fields, but who cannot intermarry.

|製作群亮相|

◆ 泰雅族

故事採集者：

里慕伊‧阿紀 Rimuy Aki

「這是當然的啦，叫我用有限的文字、插圖和註解，再引用神話故事，把泰雅族的文化介紹給大家，絕對不能夠像對自己的孩子講床邊故事一樣地輕鬆啊…」

這是她，在這次泰雅神話故事的撰寫過程裡，語重心長的體認。

「喂？親愛的馬先生，我是里慕伊，你聽聽喔：『Sgaya ta la！』要用哪些漢字，才能適當的標示發音呀？斯--卡--亞--達--辣--你覺得怎樣……」結束這通半夜打來的電話，我知道，不論任何處境，一向美美的、慵懶的里慕伊，難過的日子終於來臨了！都什麼時間了？竟然還沒——睡！

熱愛兒童教育及文字藝術的她，義不容辭的，在出版社邀稿時，十分愉悅的參與了這分工作。在編纂期間，同時進行著泰雅族母語教學及國小補救教育計劃的里慕伊，要不是自身的熱忱加上親人的「曉以大義」，我想，這工程勢必是極為嚴重的延宕(她慢條斯理的處事態度，可是出了名的)。

取消無數下午茶及電話八卦的時間，走訪各書局、圖書館、利用網路科技、蒐集種種相關資料，用對部落孩子都覺得是「不在地」的母語訪問各部落耆老，並與出版社各個有理想抱負的編輯溝通協調，再幾經無數挑燈夜戰後，終於，開了花、結了果。

花的美，我想在故事裡你會看得到；而結的果，其中過程，種種酸甜苦澀，我想只有她自己最透徹。畢竟，說這種「故事」，還是有傳承文化的使命感。

再一次，泰雅女性的智慧、毅力及美麗光芒、又在她身上展露無遺（這是她逼我一定要這樣寫的，誰叫我是她唯一的弟弟，雖然她現在已經變成了大家的「二姐」）。

鬆了一口氣…此時的里慕伊，或許正抱著血拼來的書，繼續橫躺在家中的某張躺椅上（這是她的標準配備），輕鬆的享受著沒有文化使命感的慵懶時刻吧？但她要是正好穿著一身泰雅傳統服飾的話，這種「文化遺毒」也是不錯的啦，我是說，泰雅族的神話故事，真的不錯看喔！

（本文為作者的弟弟馬紹·阿紀為里慕伊的側寫）

繪圖者：

瑁瑁·瑪邵 Meimei · Masow

「我的每一件作品都有著血濃於水的特殊感情…。」自台南家專美工科藝術設計組畢業後，瑁瑁·瑪邵從事藝術創作已十多年，其作品的圖像呈現具有十足原住民風味，她解釋自己的創作靈感源自生活經驗、祖先傳說、夢以及祖靈的庇佑…。

瑁瑁·瑪邵一直希望自己能為後生同胞留下更多的元素，可以讓他們能因此對自己的習俗祭禮、語言、古調、傳說、服飾、器物、色彩、圖騰有更多的認知與共融，所以瑁瑁·瑪邵也很熱心投入高中原住民藝術教學。雖然大家都很清楚有些施行的困難，但如何帶領新生代進入這個領域，使他們有興趣與參與感，那便是教育者要多花心思，絞盡腦汁去營造與實行。

瑁瑁·瑪邵嘗試用各種不同的素材為媒介，來詮釋自己的理念與期望，為了以藝術創作和藝術傳承服務族人，一九九八年，瑁瑁·瑪邵回歸部落從事皮革藝術、布染、公共藝術等創作與教學，陸續完成了多項公共藝術工程與多部插畫著作，例如馬武督部落的皮革藝術圖騰設計班課、台北市原住民主體公園公共藝術工程。

讀者若開車經過以藍腹鷴保育工作知名的桃園縣復興鄉高義村比亞外部落，就會看到比亞外教會旁數十公尺的彩石牆，這座護溪為主題、充滿原住民色彩的美麗游魚裝飾牆面藝術工程，就是瑁瑁·瑪邵帶領比亞外部落大學的學員完成的傑作，別忘了停下腳步來欣賞一下。

除了整日在山裡為公共藝術工程東奔西跑，瑁瑁·瑪邵在插畫創作部分也陸續完成：「一個部落到一個部落」、「看賽夏·祭矮靈」、「阿美族傳說」、「猴子與螃蟹」、「母親她束腰」、「泰雅傳說故事」及本書「泰雅族的故事插畫」，希望讓更多的朋友從本書多認識、了解原住民文化。

◆ 布農族

故事採集者：

阿浪 滿拉旺 Alang Manglavan 【漢名：杜石鑾】

他是布農族丹社群人，其部落於一九三三年日本時代被迫從南投信義鄉丹大林班地，越過平均海拔三千公尺的中央山脈，向東部遷移至花蓮，建立馬遠部落。杜石鑾是馬遠部落出生的第一代布農族人，玉里高中畢業後遠赴台北唸書，終身以當原住民公僕為職志，曾任職高雄縣原民局局長。

杜石鑾的性格就像台灣山林的石虎一樣，開朗、快樂時，笑聲很大，散發出無限的光芒。但當遇到狀況、受傷害或思考時，就變得沉默無語及無比冷靜。他平時非常重視朋友，甚至不吝惜把最好的事物都送給對方。平素喜歡原住民文化、語言、舊部落的尋根活動：除了編撰「丹群布農語」學習／教師手冊；他也是開啟台灣尋根活動的先驅，自一九八三年起，開始踏訪布農族西部丹大溪十三個舊部落，足跡踏遍中、南部的布農族舊部落。今後他希望帶動更多的人參與舊部落實地踏查，因為台灣的高山是智慧的寶庫——「與山為一，始知山」。

繪圖者：

陳景生

畫家陳景生一九三六年出生於廣東省化州市，一九六〇年畢業於廣州美術學院，師承嶺南畫派大師關山月和黎雄方。畢業後他被分配到海南島工作了二十餘年，深入黎族原住民部落區生活和工作，也對當地原住民的風土民情、民俗加以探究，成為創作上的活水源泉，這段期間的創作可說是黎族民俗繪畫期。陳景生大膽用色，活潑生動，這種重彩筆點裝飾繪畫的表現方式，實已脫離了傳統嶺南畫派風格，而創造了屬於他個人對少數民族的詮釋，用彩筆及濃重的色彩描繪原住民的純真和自然。

因緣際會下，一九九五年起陳景生旅居台灣，開始對台灣的原住民展開全心的投入探究記錄，跑遍了全島原住民部落，參與、研究各族的傳統活動，包括婚、喪、喜慶、宗教、祭典等，他用生動的畫筆為台灣原住民風土民情留下珍貴的畫作，誠屬難能可貴。

◆ 鄒族

巴蘇亞‧迪亞卡納 pasuya. Tiakiana【漢名：鄭信得】

鄭信得，牧師，嘉義縣阿里山鄒族人，1989年從神學院畢業，便返回部落。畢業當年，深受原住民自決（覺）運動思潮之影響，先後參與過多次原住民社會運動，同時對自己部落產生了新的使命感，回到部落之後，一心一意投入部落生命的延續工作。

1995年開始，關於鄒族文化生命之延續的口號，在部落裡蔓延開來──母語保存、村史整理、遷移史……鄭牧師也參與了其中多項鄒族文化復振的工作，包括阿里山鄉誌編撰助理（1996 - 1998）、《鄒訊》主編（1995 - 2001）、鄒語工作室的鄒語教材研發編製等。

另外，鄭牧師亦把經年累月的自助文化研究蒐集的資料，透過學術機構、報導文學徵文比賽、論文、報告等方式呈現，盡心盡力於鄒族文化的傳承。

阿伐伊‧尤于伐那 Avai 'e Yoifana【漢名：莊暉明】

早年在外求學，畢業於正修工專電子工程科，服役後回山上務農。從小受姨丈尚可先生（國中教師，已故）繪畫薰陶，原本只是閒暇之餘作畫自娛，後來為響應提升原住民傳統文化技藝的活動，投入鄒族藝術繪畫工作。

除了繪畫，也嘗試音樂創作，並自組樂團，試圖結合鄒族傳統音樂與現代流行音樂，創作出屬於鄒族「現代音樂」的曲風，並藉著演出，來歌詠鄒族之美。此外，也常去山林狩獵，目的不是獵物，而是循著先人的足跡，親身體會祖先堅忍的精神與大自然的力量，以取得創作靈感。

期望藉著一件件創作作品，能感動族人與外界，重視鄒族這一支慢慢被現代文明、商業利益埋沒的民族。

新自然主義